MARA'S MOVE

Other books by Jean C. Gordon:

Other books in this series:
Candy Kisses

Mandy and the Mayor
Love Undercover
Bachelor Father

MARA'S MOVE

•

Jean C. Gordon

AVALON BOOKS
NEW YORK

042909

F
Goy

Published by Thomas Bouregy & Co., Inc.
160 Madison Avenue, New York, NY 10016

Library of Congress Cataloging-in-Publication Data

Gordon, Jean C.
    Mara's move / Jean C. Gordon.
        p.   cm.
    ISBN 978-0-8034-9955-3
    I. Title

PS3557.06682M37   2009
813'.54—dc22
                                                2008052526

PRINTED IN THE UNITED STATES OF AMERICA
ON ACID-FREE PAPER
BY HADDON CRAFTSMEN, BLOOMSBURG, PENNSYLVANIA

Much thanks to BFS—you know who you are.

Chapter One

No! No! No! This was so not happening again.

Mara Riley gulped her drink, her eyes glued to the scene playing out across the sports bar. Her boyfriend was nuzzling the neck of some leggy blond. Was *she* the reason their dates had all been places they were unlikely to run into anyone from work? And here she'd thought he was being romantic, wanting her all to himself. "Hey, isn't that Ross?" her coworker Caro asked, pointing across the dance floor.

Mara struggled not to choke on the ice in her mouth.

"That must be his wife—or it had better be." Caro laughed.

Mara crunched down hard on the cube, possibly cracking one of the few fillings she had. Wife? Ross is married? And how did Caro know if she didn't. This was worse than last time. Luke had only been engaged.

I'm not a stupid woman. How could I have not known he was married? Mara tore her cocktail napkin into little pieces. *Uh, maybe because he never gave any sign he was taken. The rat.*

"He used to be a real player," Caro said. "Before *and* after the wedding." Her voice lowered. "He and his wife separated for a while, but I heard they recently reconciled."

If he was separated when they went out it wasn't *that* bad. Mara swallowed the bile that rose in her throat. "You know his wife?" she asked, thankful that the music hid the squeak in her voice.

"My sister works with her." Caro studied the couple. "I thought she was a redhead, but I suppose she could have bleached her hair. I bet that's not his wife, though. I'll have to ask my sister."

This was getting worse and worse. Mara dropped the last of the napkin onto the small pile in front of her. "I'd better get going." She pushed away from the table.

Her coworker looked at the paper pile on the table in front of Mara. Her eyes narrowed. "It's early yet."

Mara felt the flush creeping up her neck. Did Caro suspect her interest—make that her former interest—in Ross? That would be just great. She wouldn't be able to show her face at work. She'd look as stupid as she felt.

"I haven't finished the activity schedules for tomorrow," Mara said. It wasn't exactly a lie. She hadn't. But then, she usually wrote them the first thing in the morning. Her boss didn't care as long as they were posted for the guests by nine o'clock. "I really should get back to my room and do them."

"Okay." Caro shrugged. "See you tomorrow."

Mara weaved her way through the crowd that was just starting to fill the bar and emerged in Glenhaven's main lobby. A crystal chandelier salvaged from some long-ago demolished, antebellum home twinkled above. But the feature that drew her most were the large carved oak doors at the far end. She sized up the room. Fifty steps between her and escape. If she could make it across the lobby without running into anyone she knew and get through the doors, she'd be outside where she could cry or laugh, whatever it took to vent her frustration and personal embarrassment.

She pasted a smile on her face and forged ahead. *Forty seven, forty eight, forty nine, fifty.* With a twist of the door knob and a push, she was outside. The humid air hit her like a wet dishrag. April was early for this kind of heat and humidity, even in North Carolina. She breathed the heavy air. Too hot to run off her anger and frustration. But maybe she could stomp off some of it crossing the lawn to her room.

The cool air that greeted her when she opened the annex door offered welcome relief. She tramped down the hall. The functionality of the annex contrasted sharply with the understated opulence of the resort itself. But her room was comfortable—and home for now. She let herself in, switched on the light, and tossed her bag on the sofa bed she hadn't bothered to fold up this morning. After grabbing a bottle of water from her minifridge, she settled crossed legged on the mattress with her laptop.

MaraNara: <Candy?>

Mara hit enter and sent the message to her best friend.

Priceless: <hey>
MaraNara: <i'm an idiot>
Priceless: <???>
MaraNara: <ross. he's married>
Priceless: <the rat! but it's not like you were really going out>
MaraNara: <i know, i know, but i thought he had potential>
Priceless: <true>
MaraNara: <my mother has stunted my ability to see men for what they are>
Priceless: <the attorney/doctor thing>
MaraNara: <yep. to prove her wrong, i always pick losers with a capital L>
Priceless: <you have had a bad streak>
MaraNara: <you had the right idea. i'm swearing off men and concentrating all of my energy on my career>

Priceless: <i didn't exactly swear off men, only being fixed up with my brothers' friends>

MaraNara: <same thing. the only men you had time to meet outside of your job were the blind dates Price, Price & Price, Ltd set up>

Priceless: <not like it was my choice. stacey expected me to be on 24/7>

MaraNara: <how is the boss from Hades?>

Priceless: <FORMER boss. alive and well in DC, emailing me way too often>

MaraNara: <and mike?>

MaraNara: <and the wedding plans?>

Priceless: <great and great>

MaraNara: <thx for giving me veto power over the bridesmaids' dresses>

Priceless: <you're my best friend and after your sister's orange blossom extravaganza you deserved a choice>

MaraNara: <::::shudder:::: don't remind me>

Priceless: <okay then. let me tell you what my brother wants us to do>

MaraNara: <which one?>

Mara did a visual inventory of Candy's older brothers. All three of them were hunky, but irritating, to Candy at least.

Priceless: <alex>

Against her will, Mara's heart did a triple beat, shades of the school girl crush she'd had on Candy's next older brother. He really was the cutest, blond and athletic, and less smothering of Candy than the other two.

MaraNara: <alex is in on the wedding planning?>
Priceless: <he wants to give us his "honeymoon" cruise>
MaraNara: <???>
Priceless: <the one She Who Will Not Be Named picked out for their honeymoon>
MaraNara: <for real?>
Priceless: <for real. this is one of my brothers we're talking about. it's all paid for. he doesn't want it to go to waste. but we're going to Ireland.>
MaraNara: <yeah!>
Priceless: <who would have thought that social-climbing SWWNBN would have broken her engagement to an up-and-coming attorney like Alex for a back-to-nature forest-ranger type?>
MaraNara: <i know! that must have been some kind of interesting guided hike she and alex went on. maybe you could send me the travel brochure.>
Priceless: <i'll put alex right on it.>
MaraNara: <nope i don't go there.>
Priceless: <come on that was high school.>
MaraNara: <yeah & i made an even bigger fool of myself over alex than I have over ross.>

Mara glanced at her computer clock.

MaraNara: <i'd better get going. gotta get up early and conquer the world of hotel management. hope i don't lose it if i see ross.>
Priceless: <you won't>
MaraNara: <wish you were here>
Priceless: <me too>
MaraNara: <UC has a good law school>
Priceless: <yeah, your point?>
MaraNara: <you could come down here for school>
Priceless: <and about mike?>
MaraNara: <bring him too ☺>
Priceless: <you'll be fine>
MaraNara: <i know>
Priceless: <talk tomorrow>
MaraNara: <bye>
Priceless: <bye>

Mara stared at the blank message box. She was happy that Candy had Mike. She'd helped fix them up. But she missed commiserating with Candy about the sad state of dating. Mara shut down the computer and switched on the TV before settling in for the night.

She rubbed her temples, trying to get rid of the dull ache. She'd stayed up too late last night watching British comedies on PBS and hadn't slept well afterward. But, at least the morning had started out okay. She hadn't run into Ross. If life was at all fair, she wouldn't have to face him today . . . tomorrow . . . the rest of the week.

"Mara, could I talk with you?" her boss Nan asked.

"Sure. Should I finish these schedules first?"

"No, they can wait." Nan's serious expression didn't bode well. Normally, she was a regular Little Mary Sunshine.

Mara slipped the schedules into her to-do box on the desk. *Could Nan know about Ross? How lame. There was nothing to know.* Mara followed Nan into her office.

"Sit, please." Nan motioned to a chair on the other side of the desk and picked up a pen. She began to flick it slowly between her thumb and forefinger. "I'm not sure how to start. I know I said when you were promoted to assistant activity director that after three months, you'd be made permanent."

The pen flicks increased in tempo and Mara's heart picked up the beat. Her probationary period was supposed to be up at the end of this week. She'd officially be Glenhaven's assistant activity director. But it sure didn't sound like that was going to happen. Mara's mind raced through how she could have messed up and couldn't come up with anything, unless she'd been really obvious about her former interest in Ross.

"I told you we had to keep the position open for my former assistant, in case she decided she wanted to come back after she had her baby, that she hadn't officially re-signed."

Each word came faster than the one before, as if building crescendo for the final chord. *No job for you.*

Nan put the pen down and placed her hands flat on the desk. "I never thought she would. But she's coming back next Monday. I'm sorry."

"Where does that leave me? I *did* resign my job in registration to take this one." Mara couldn't believe how calm she sounded. She wanted to scream, *I'm eight hundred miles from my closest friends and family and I don't even have a place to live if I'm not a Glenhaven employee.*

"There's another job open. It's not exactly in your field." Nan stopped.

"O-kay. What is it?" As long as it wasn't back at the front desk, she could be open.

"Public relations."

"You're right. Not my field."

"I think you'd be good."

Mara studied Nan's face. Was she for real? Or just covering herself?

"Yeah? English wasn't my favorite subject."

"This job is a lot more than press releases. You'd be kind of a secret shopper for corporate."

"I'd be ratting out other employees?"

Nan frowned. "No, that's not the point. You'd be checking out the various resorts, hotels, restaurants, and other facilities as a guest and coming up with ideas for improving and promoting the services."

"Sort of like a perpetual vacation."

"Well, you would have to write reports and recommendations on your findings and between reviews help with promo projects, along with some administrative duties."

"Administrative duties like typing and filing?" She knew there had to be a downside. The rest of the job sounded too good to be true.

"Pretty much. You'd have to maintain reports, type press releases."

Mara flexed her fingers. A little typing wouldn't kill her.

"And whatever else the PR director needs."

Alarms went off in Mara's head. *Whatever* sounded dangerously close to the gofer job her friend Candy had had with the gubernatorial campaign.

"What's the PR director like?"

"Mellow. You'll like him."

Mara relaxed her grip on the chair arms. Candy's old boss couldn't be described by anyone as anything near mellow.

"So, do I apply through HR?"

"Nope. I've already put your name in for the job."

Mara knew that Nan was being helpful. That she felt bad about having to let her go. But going ahead and recommending her for the PR job kind of put her in a spot. No, she was in a spot anyway. No job and no place to live.

"I understand if you need a little time to decide. Interviews are running through Friday."

Two days away. Little was right. "No. I'll give it a try."

"Great." Nan clapped her hands together. "Your interview is just a formality. Glenhaven likes to take care of its own. So current employees always have preference, and I've given you an excellent reference."

"Thanks." *I think.*

"Oh, I didn't tell you." Nan's eyes lit up.

There was more?

"You start off with a five-day cruise to check out the Carolina Lines' newly revamped hosted singles cruises. They have special activities for the single people onboard. Kind of a subcruise within the cruise. The Lines are ready to kick off a big promotion for them."

"A job that starts out with a cruise? I could handle that." Sun, ready-made food, men. No, scratch the men. She was all career now. "Then what?"

"After the cruise, you'd be working out of corporate headquarters."

"So, I'll need to get a place in Ashville." A new start away from Glenhaven resort might be just what she needed.

"Yeah, but the pay is higher if that's your concern."

"No, more that I've gotten used to being able to dash off to work at the last minute and the convenience of no commute home." She grinned at her boss.

Nan returned her smile. "Your interview is first thing tomorrow morning." She handed Mara a Glenhaven business card with writing on the back.

"I'll be there."

Mara finished the rest of the day on automatic pilot, skipping her usual lunch with coworkers and leaving as soon as her shift was done. Back in her room, she booted her laptop.

Darn! Candy wasn't online. Mara would have liked to talk with her about her career change.

She checked her email. Six alerts about some hot new stock, four more spam mails for male mood enhancers, and her blog feeds. As she clicked to delete the junk mail, a new message appeared. Her mother's weekly inquisition and family news. She skimmed the email. Her sister and her doctor husband were looking for a bigger house. No surprise there. A paragraph about how wonderfully her brother-in-law treated Kate. Translation: He gives her lots of money to spend.

The usual questions followed. How is work? Translation: Are you ready to come home and seriously start looking for a husband? Have you met anyone interesting? Translation: Any eligible lawyers or doctors to take you away from your piddling little job? How are Candy's wedding plans coming? Translation: Look, even *she* found someone who will at least help take care of her, although she could have done better.

Mara's fingers itched to respond not to worry about her making a bad marriage match. She'd met someone new and he was already married. And she'd gotten rid of that nasty little job. She closed the email program. She'd deal with Mom later, when she was in a better frame of mind.

"Candy, where are you?" she asked the screen when her IM friends list showed she still wasn't online. Mara minimized IM and opened her Internet browser. She Googled "Glenhaven Corporation" "public relations" and a list of GHC links appeared. Might as well find out what she was getting herself into.

Chapter Two

*W*as that Alex Price lugging a suitcase up the ramp to the Carolina? Mara squinted against the bright morning sun. *Yep, it sure was. What was he doing here in Charleston? Candy hadn't said anything about him coming down.*

"Alex!" She waved.

The blond man raised his hand to shield the sun and looked up into the crowd. He frowned.

"Alex!" She called again. This time he saw her. Their eyes met briefly before he stopped short and glanced behind him as if to size up the opportunity to turn around and escape back down the ramp. *What was with that?*

"Excuse me."

Mara stepped back to let some other travelers pass. Once they were by, she looked back down the gangway, but didn't see Alex. Had he really left? They'd avoided each other for years, ever since her freshman year in high school when she'd chased him relentlessly. Heat crept into her cheeks. He'd gotten really good at maneuvering the halls of Harmony Hills High without her spotting him. But they were adults now. Time to get over it. She turned her back to the gangway and went off in search of her cabin.

Alex turned back up the gangway. Great! His sister's best friend. He'd come on this trip to get away from family and friends. Six months of their well-meaning sympathy was as much as he could take. He shrugged off a pang of regret. He was *so* over his ex-fiancé. But this would have been his honeymoon cruise. He picked up his pace so he wouldn't be blocking the people behind him.

Mara was here. So what? She was probably with some guy. It wasn't like she was going to tag after him like she did when she was a kid. He lifted his hand to shield his eyes from the sun. Mara had cut her hair. The light breeze blew the wispy, dark curls in a riotous halo around her face. She used to wear her hair long. He didn't much like short hair on women. But on Mara, the short, no-nonsense cut looked right. His gaze drifted lower. The silky-looking sleeveless shirt and fitted Capri pants suited her too. If she wasn't his little sister's best friend, almost like another sister, he wouldn't mind her tagging after him now.

What was he thinking? This was Mara, little Mara. That would be his mantra for the cruise. Little Mara. Only Mara wasn't little anymore. He forced himself to think of his ex-fiancé Laura. He could barely make himself conjure up her likeness. But he had no trouble reliving the pain and embarrassment and remembering his personal vow to steer clear of any female contacts that could lead to anything more than a casual hookup. His entire family would kill him if he put the moves on Mara.

When Alex reached the top of the gangway, Mara was gone. A uniformed woman smiled at him. "Welcome to the *Carolina*. Enjoy your cruise." He looked at the crowd on the deck. With any luck, he and Mara might not even run into each other. He headed down the deck and up the elevator to his room. Getting away from the bustle of everyone boarding would be good.

He unlocked the door and stepped in. When the cruise line said minisuite, they meant mini. The room was somewhat smaller than many hotel rooms he'd stayed in. Laura wouldn't have been impressed. He walked across the thickly carpeted cabin. The cabin might be small, but the balcony gave him his own space away from the other travelers. He walked out into the sunlight and tested the deck chair. Not bad. The small umbrella attached to the back provided the right amount of shade. He leaned back, crossed his legs, and surveyed the deck below through the intricate curls of the wrought-iron railing.

A small figure with curly dark hair caught his eye.

Mara? Alex smiled to himself, then shook his head. He had to decide whether he wanted to seek out Mara because she was Mara and a family friend, or avoid her. Or he'd drive himself crazy. He checked his watch. He had a couple of hours to relax before his assigned dinner time.

Mara rushed into the dining room, anxious to see if cruise food lived up to its reputation. The tour of the kitchens she'd taken earlier had certainly held a lot of promise. Her stomach grumbled at the memory of the yummy-smelling fruit turnovers the pastry chefs had been preparing. She should have had more than a power bar for lunch.

"Can I help you find your table?" one of the hostesses asked.

"Please. It's table seven."

Mara followed the statuesque blond across the dining room.

"Here you are." She motioned toward a table with a metal placard engraved with a seven. Several people were seated with their backs toward her.

"Thanks." Mara smiled at the hostess.

She smiled in return. "Enjoy."

So far, the dining room was scoring high. She walked around to the other side of the table and came face to face with Alex.

"Imagine meeting you here." She forced a smile this time.

"Um. So that *was* you."

"Yep, the crazy lady waving and shouting your name down the gangway. That was me."

"I thought it might be, but you were gone before I got to the top of the gangway."

Um, yeah, it didn't seem worthwhile hanging around for a guy who looked like he'd rather go overboard than run into me.

"We should get together sometime and catch up," she said, wondering now whether he had really gone into his disappearing act or she'd imagined it because that's what she'd expected from him.

"Yeah, sure."

Was that a yeah sure, let's get together or a yeah sure, whatever brush off? Jeez. He was getting to her without even trying, even though she had moved way beyond any first love feelings—real or imagined—she might have once had for Alex.

Mara walked around the table and took a seat several place settings away from Alex. Distance is good.

"And who do we have here?" tall, tanned, and gorgeous next to her asked with an inviting smile.

Her gaze moved down past his broad shoulders over his Polo shirt to his long, tapered fingers. No wedding ring. A smaller hand flashing a sparkling wedding set slid over his sleeve and twined fingers with his. The owner of that hand leaned forward to be seen. Her heated stare skewered and roasted Mara before she could even open her mouth.

No going there, even if TTG had been flirting.

"I'm Drew Fields," he said. The smaller hand squeezed his. He winced. "And this is my wife, Christie."

"Mara Riley."

He favored her with what could have been a mind-melting smile if he were available and she hadn't sworn off men.

"Hi," Christie said. "We're on our honeymoon."

"Congratulations," Mara said.

Christie gave her a tight-lipped smile.

Mara picked up her water glass and took a sip. Okay, so you congratulate the man. What was it you were supposed to say to the woman? With all the engagement and married etiquette her mother had drummed into her, you'd think she'd know automatically.

Mara turned back to the couple. They were deep in quiet conversation. She glanced at the empty chair on her other side, but avoided looking across the table at Alex. She might as well do her job. The hostess who had shown her to the table had been friendly and helpful. She discreetly examined her silverware and water glass. Both were spotless. The forest-green napkins were folded attractively next to the ivory-stoneware coffee cups.

"Hi."

Mara looked up to see a voluptuous blond who barely looked legal.

"I'm Tiffani, with two *i*'s," she announced to the group, flipping her waist-length hair over her shoulder before settling into the seat beside Alex.

Christie, Drew, Mara, and Alex all introduced themselves.

"We're going to go get drinks," Drew said. "Can I get anyone something?"

"I'm good," Alex said.

"Something fruity for me." Tiffani smiled up at Drew.

Mara waited for her to start batting her heavily mascaraed lashes, but to her credit she didn't.

"How about you, Mara?"

"I'll wait for coffee. Thanks."

Once Drew and Christie had left, Tiffani looked from Mara to Alex. "So, are you all singles?" she asked with a big smile.

That's cutting to the chase, Mara thought. Maybe she should give that a try. Find out right off whether a guy's married, engaged, or otherwise taken.

"Pardon?" Alex asked.

"You know, the singles thing."

Confusion clouded Alex's hazel eyes.

"Hosted singles," Mara explained for Tiffani. "It's a special deal for people who are cruising alone. You sign up ahead of time. It's supposed to make it easier to mix and meet people."

"No." He shook his head. "I came by myself to get away. I deal with people enough at work."

"Oh, that's too bad," Tiffani said, oblivious to his response. "There's a big singles party later."

Alex turned to Mara. "Are you part of this singles thing?"

"Yep." She smiled at Tiffani. "The party should be fun."

His eyes narrowed and he puckered his lips.

"Maybe we could get you in," Tiffani offered. "Do you know if we can bring dates?"

Alex's expression turned even more sour.

Since when was Alex Price averse to a little partying? Had his ex-fiancé done that much of a job on him?

"I don't think we're supposed to bring anyone who's not signed up."

Tiffani pouted. "I thought since we'd be eating together and all, like family, we'd get friendly and want to hang out together."

Like family. Where had this girl come from? She didn't know any of them, whether they had anything in common. And since when did being family mean you wanted to hang together? Except, maybe, the Prices. They were close, not like Mara and her mother and Kate.

From the way Tiffani was devouring Alex with her eyes, it was obvious Alex was the one she wanted to hang with. Not that Mara could blame her. Alex was a babe magnet without even trying—or knowing he was. Incredibly blond hair slightly in need of a trim. Blue eyes that sparked with a hint of mischief. Subtle laugh lines that said he enjoyed life. And from the fit of his oxford shirt, sitting in a law office all day hadn't softened the muscular physique that, back in high school, had helped put him on the all-state lacrosse team two years in a row.

Yep, he certainly wasn't hard on the eyes. She dragged herself away from her appraisal before he caught her staring. "There are lots of other activities where you and Alex could get together."

Alex cut short a strangled cough with a quick gulp of water.

"Are you okay?" Tiffani asked, patting him on the back.

"Fine. I'm fine." He finished off his water and shot Mara a black look.

Watching Alex squirm was kind of fun. It reminded Mara of the time she and Candy had caught Alex slipping into his room in the early hours of the morning after he'd told his father he'd be home by midnight. They just happened to still be awake in Candy's room listening to music and talking. Keeping their mouths shut had earned them a ride to school with Alex for a month, which sure beat taking the bus. Alex had ended up earning points with his dad for being so nice to his sister.

Tiffani twisted a long blond strand of hair around her finger. "So, what do you all do? I just finished my associate degree in January. It took me an extra semester with cheerleading and all."

Mara refrained from rolling her eyes.

"I'm planning on going into PR." Tiffani let the lock unfurl into a long spiral curl.

Hmmm, Mara thought. If this was the competition, maybe she should stay with PR instead of hotel management.

"Mom and Dad gave me this cruise as a graduation present."

God, was I ever that young? Mara swirled the ice in her goblet. *No, not even when I was that young.*

"That's decent," Alex said.

Better than decent. Mara placed the goblet back on the table. Her mother hadn't even come to her baccalaureate or graduate degree ceremony, let alone reward her for her hard work. Mother Dearest had still been angry that Mara hadn't done as she'd said and taken a one-year medical assistant or paralegal course to set her up to snag a doctor or attorney husband. Mara had had other ideas and she'd pursued them with no help from her mother.

"Your turn." Tiffani smiled at Alex.

"I'm an attorney."

"Like 'Law and Order'?"

Mara laughed. "More like 'Desperate Housewives.'"

"Huh?"

"Very funny." Alex drew his lips into a thin line. "I handle more divorces and civil suits than criminal cases," he answered Tiffani.

"How did Mara . . . ?" Tiffani's eyes lit up. "You guys already know each other."

"Guilty," Mara said.

"Mara is my little sister's best friend."

Tiffani eyed Alex. "You're not here together, are you? You said you're not signed up for the singles' activities." She zeroed-in on Mara. "And you said you are."

He dismissed the question with a laugh. "No, we're not together."

Jeez, he didn't have to make it sound so farfetched.

"Yeah, I haven't seen Alex in ages. It was a complete surprise when I saw him boarding." And trying to unboard.

"And you just happened to end up at the same dinner table?" Tiffani asked. "What a coincidence."

"Or not," Alex muttered.

"What? You think I somehow set this up?" Mara shook out her napkin. Hard. And smoothed it on her lap.

"You work for the corporation that owns the cruise line. Or you did," he said.

Mara chipped at a crack in her nail. "I still do."

"Cool," Tiffani said, oblivious to the tension crackling between Mara and Alex. "Did you win the trip or get a big discount or something?"

"Yeah, something like that," Mara answered. "But I'm a guest on the cruise just like you guys."

More or less.

She looked directly at Alex. "I couldn't have arranged our dinner seating even if I had wanted to. And I didn't. I learned my lesson about you long ago."

He winced and shifted in his seat.

Good. He should be uncomfortable considering the last—and only—dinner she'd arranged that had included him. Mara had thought having a couples-only dinner party would be a sophisticated way to celebrate Alex's high school graduation and get something going with him before he left for college. Then, he'd shown up with another girl. Totally humiliating.

Drew and Christie returned, followed by an older man dressed in crisp khakis and a Polo shirt.

"This is Jack," Drew introduced the man. "He's our missing diner." Drew motioned to the empty seat next to Mara. "This is Mara and Tiffani and Alex."

"Hi," Tiffani and Mara said. Alex nodded.

"We picked Jack up on our way back to the table," Christie smiled at him over her shoulder and slipped into her seat. "I overheard him asking the hostess where table seven was."

Drew frowned.

Trouble in paradise? Mara couldn't blame Christie for looking and smiling. Jack wasn't bad for an older guy, not bad at all. She glanced sideways at him as he walked around her to take the empty seat. Broad shoulders. Silver-threaded black hair. Trim physique. Deck shoes, no socks. Not bad at all. Why couldn't she pick up someone like that—in a younger model?

"Is that my drink?" Tiffani asked.

"What? Yeah." Drew handed her a tall glass with a multicolored straw and the stereotypical umbrella perched on the side.

"Thanks, it looks yummy." Tiffani's gazed darted from Alex to Jack, and Mara wasn't sure if she meant the drink or the men. They were pretty yummy.

Jack was the dark and mysterious night to Alex's

open sunny day. Sunny, except for the black looks he'd been favoring her with all evening and his uncharacteristically sour and unfriendly attitude. He was making Jack's aloofness appear warm and fuzzy.

"We didn't miss the server, did we?" Drew asked. "I'm starved."

As if on cue, their server appeared. "Are you ready to order?" He placed a napkin-covered basket on the table.

"Yes," Alex answered for them.

Mara picked up the menu and checked out the choices again while the others ordered.

"We'll have the lobster special for two," Drew said.

Tiffani asked about substituting rice for the potato that came with the grilled salmon special and a different vegetable for the salad before deciding on a Cobb salad.

Alex and Jack rattled off exactly what they wanted. No hesitation or questions, right down to how they wanted their filet mignon cooked and their choice of salad dressing.

The server turned to Mara.

"I'll have scallops Marcella with french fries and blue cheese dressing on my salad."

The server jotted down her order and left.

"Are you sure that's safe?" Alex asked. "I can get our server back."

Everyone stared at him.

"Why wouldn't it be?" Was there some kind of recall on scallops that she'd missed? She was relatively up on current events. The Glenhaven Restaurant hadn't had any problem serving them last week.

Alex cleared his throat. "Candy's sixteenth birthday party."

Obviously, that was a hint. But of what? The Prices were big on birthday parties. She'd gone to Candy's every year since they were about six. Alex's too, and T.J.'s and Jason's.

"We went to Lakeview Manor. You ordered scallops," he coached.

Mara shook her head. "It's not registering."

He glanced around the table. Then he mouthed, "You got sick."

"Oh, yeah!"

He leaned forward on his elbows. "You said you were having a reaction to the scallops. That you were sensitive to some kinds of seafood."

"Urn, I did. I'm not."

"What?"

Mara folded back the napkin on the basket the server had left and took a slice of warm bread. "I was getting over the flu." She concentrated on spreading butter on the slice. "I had told my mother I was feeling fine. If she'd found out or your dad knew why I was sick, I wouldn't have been able to go skiing the next day with your family."

"Quick thinking," Drew complimented her.

Alex just shook his head.

"I was fine the next day. Had a great time. It was the only skiing I got in that winter." She looked him in the eye and took a bite of the bread.

He blinked.

She chewed. Despite the butter, the bread was dry and tasteless. And her water was gone. The server should have topped it up. She'd have to remember to put that in her report. This job would be a lot easier if she could carry her checklist around with her.

"Do you still ski?" Jack asked.

"No." Mara's college years flashed by. Overfull schedule. Waitressing every night to pay the bills. "I haven't had the time. Maybe once I'm settled in Asheville."

"Asheville? You might enjoy some of our local runs." Jack's drawl was like maple syrup. Smooth and sweet and not too thick.

"You're from Asheville?"

"Born and bred."

Mara resisted an unladylike snort at his clichéd answer. "The local resorts have good skiing?" She waited for him to expound on the great trails like the hometown boy—man—whatever he was.

"I prefer the Rockies," he said. "Ever ski Aspen?"

Hmmm. That was a surprise.

"No. Lake Placid is as challenging as I've done."

"What's wrong with Lake Placid?" Alex asked.

"Ah, a New Yorker," Jack said.

That voice again. Mara wondered if she could bottle it.

"Mara's a New Yorker too."

What was with Alex? He'd never been gung ho on New York. In fact, he'd gone to law school in Maryland. Candy had been sure he'd end up practicing in D.C.

"Was," she said. "I've been in North Carolina about a year now."

"I'm from Pennsylvania," Tiffani chimed in, drawing Jack's attention. "And I've never skied."

"You should give it a try," he said.

"Oh, I don't know, I'm not into cold. I stay inside as much as possible during the winter." She gave a fake shiver.

Jack chuckled.

"I'm with you," Drew said, draping his arm over the back of Christie's chair. "We're more beach than snow people."

Alex leaned back in his chair, crossed his arms, and smirked at Mara as if he'd just orchestrated some kind of coup by diverting the conversation and Jack's attention from her. She might think he was jealous if she didn't know the Price brothers' propensity for overprotecting their sister Candy—and her by association.

"Yep. Sand, sea, and sun," Tiffani said. "That's why I'm here. And to meet new people." She grinned at each of them, allowing her rose-tinted lips to curve into a full smile for Alex.

He reached for the bread basket before her gaze could catch his.

Ha! Looks like Alex has a new BFF. Mara popped the last bite of her bread into her mouth.

Tiffani's smile dimmed, but only slightly. "Mara and I are going to the singles' party tonight. Are you signed up?" she asked Jack.

"No, I hadn't planned on it." Jack tented his fingers. "This is kind of a working vacation for me."

"Me—" Mara stopped herself before she blurted out *too* and blew her cover. "Erm. How's that?"

"I'm with Glenhaven Corp.'s legal department and I'm teaching an onboard seminar on estate planning."

"Hey," Tiffani said, "Alex is a lawyer too."

"Is that right?"

"Yep, but he's more into divorces, wills, that sort of stuff," she said.

Jack looked down his nose at Alex.

"There's nothing wrong with family law," Alex snapped.

Oh, ho, were they going to duke it out at the table? Mara thought twenty-first century men had gotten past work as the total definition of their being. Then again, Jack was probably more a twentieth-century man.

She spotted their server and deflected the conversation. "Ah, here are our dinners."

None too soon for Alex. His brothers were all whipped on corporate and commercial litigation too. Thought the family-law part of their practice was okay for fill-in billing when nothing more interesting was available. Alex thought family law *was* interesting and wasn't in a mood to argue that point with Mr. Smooth or Mara.

"So, Jack," Mara said, "you work at Glenhaven Corporate in Asheville?"

Alex tuned out Jack's answer and dug into his steak with a vengeance and the goal of splitting as quickly as he could without giving himself indigestion. To be fair to his dinner companions, he knew they weren't irritating him on purpose but he was irritated just the same. He'd thought the cruise might help him get out of the funk he'd been in the past few months, but he'd brought the funk with him.

"Are you finished, sir?" the server asked.

Alex stared at his empty plate and couldn't recall tasting a single bite of his food. "Yes, I am."

The server cleared their plates and offered coffee and dessert.

"No, thanks," Alex said. This dinner had to have been one of the longest he had ever endured, and he'd attended some excruciatingly long bar association dinners. He had to admit, though, that watching Mara across the table in her clingy little scooped neck top was a lot more pleasant than having boring discussions with his bar association colleagues—and much more frustrating.

He wouldn't have minded catching up with her. That is, if he'd been able to get a word in edgewise. Between Tiffani's chatter and Jack's monopolizing Mara with Glenhaven this and Glenhaven that, he hadn't had a chance. And when Mara had talked to him, the talk had consisted mainly of pointed jabs aimed at him.

He stood. "I'll see you all later."

"At the party?"

There Tiffani went again. He wasn't in any kind of mood to go to a singles meat market.

But before he could say so, Tiffani wheedled, "C'mon, come to the party. It'll be fun."

Alex's shoulders stiffened and his gaze met Mara's. Not in this lifetime.

Chapter Three

Mara took a final sip of the coffee she hadn't wanted. Everyone else was gone—finally. Now she could grade the table cleanup. She placed the cup on the saucer, scratched a few comments in her notebook, and closed it with a soft snap.

She had time before she had to get ready for the singles' mixer. If she could pick up the WiFi on her personal digital assistant, maybe she could find out what Alex was doing on her cruise and why he had a bug up his behind.

Mara walked out to the Promenade deck lounge and settled on a couch in the back. She powered up her Blackberry, tapped the messaging program icon with the stylus, and waited for her friends list to appear. The program was taking forever to open. She wiggled her toes in her too-tight Manolo Blahnik shoes. She knew she should have gotten a half-size larger, but they were on sale, and this was the only pair left in black. The multicolored circle continued to spin on the screen. This connection was slower than dial up.

She reached in her bag for her notebook to see if Internet use was one of the things she was supposed to report on. A neatly folded cocktail napkin fell out of the front pocket. *Weird.* It could *not* have tumbled off the table into the pocket of her bag all neat and folded. She picked the paper up.

Drinks at 11 in the Lido Lounge? was scrawled across the white paper followed by a bold *Drew*.

Mara crumpled the napkin into a ball, closed her eyes, and dropped her head on the couch back. *Why me?* She lifted her head and checked the Blackberry screen.

Priceless: <Mara?>

Mara slid the little keyboard out and typed.

MaraNara: <help! do I have an S tattooed on my forehead that I can't see?>
Priceless: <???>
MaraNara: <like for skank?>
Priceless: <you're not>
MaraNara: <then, why do I attract all these men who want to cheat on their women?>

Priceless: <ross? that's way over.>
MaraNara: <no, never mind.>

She had better things to talk about than that skeeze Drew. Poor Christie.

Priceless: <ok. so how's the cruise so far?>
MaraNara: <about the cruise>
Priceless: <yeah?>
MaraNara: <guess who I ran into.>
Priceless: <someone from work?>
MaraNara: <actually, yes, but someone else we both know.>
Priceless: <from school?>
MaraNara: <nope. alex.>
Priceless: <that's where he went?>
MaraNara: <you didn't know?>
Priceless: <nope, he just told dad he was going on vacation.>
MaraNara: <wait! this is the honeymoon cruise he was trying to give you.>
Priceless: <yep. he was supposed to be married this past Saturday>
MaraNara: <maybe that's why he's acting weird>
Priceless: <he's always a little weird>
MaraNara: <no, more than usual. first he tried to avoid me.>

Priceless: <that's not new>

MaraNara: <true, but then at dinner, he acted almost jealous when I was talking to the lawyer from GHC.>

Priceless: <alex had dinner with you?>

MaraNara: <we're assigned the same table>

Priceless: <with a guy from GHC?>

MaraNara: <yeah, some corporate attorney or something.>

Priceless: <you don't want to go there. take my word for it. all those blind dates with my brothers' friends. corporate lawyers :::shudder::::>

MaraNara: <he's older anyway, but not bad. kind of attractive in a Pierce Brosnan sort of way.>

Priceless: <your mother would love it. you start off your cruise having dinner with two eligible lawyers.>

MaraNara: <and a barely twenty-something blond chickie who wants to be alex's and my new best friend.>

Priceless: <LOL>

MaraNara: <and a newlywed couple. HE asked me out for drinks later.>

Priceless: <ah, the *s* on your forehead.>

MaraNara: <yeah. i'm ignoring him. the chickie and I are going to a singles party tonight.>

Priceless: <?!?.>

MaraNara: <it's part of the job.>

Priceless: <some people have it sooo tough. is alex going too?>

MaraNara: <no. he didn't sign up for the singles events, said he wants to get away from people.>

Priceless: <he went on a cruise to get away from people?>

MaraNara: <I told you. weird.>

Priceless: <way weird. are you sure this is our Alex?>

MaraNara: <or an alex pod person.>

Priceless: <I knew laura did a real number on him, but . . . >

MaraNara: <maybe he'll snap out of it by dinner tomorrow.>

Priceless: <keep me posted.>

MaraNara: <don't worry.>

Priceless: <he's been kind of depressed when he's not being mad.>

MaraNara: <I'll make sure he doesn't jump ship.>

Priceless: <don't say that. there was just another news story today.>

MaraNara: <I was kidding.>

Priceless: <I know. but he's been weird here at home too.>

MaraNara: <so chickie and I will hang out with him if he'll let us.>

Priceless: <he's not ready to get involved with anyone.>

MaraNara: <not to worry. I detected NO interest at all on his part.>

He *hadn't* been interested, had he? Mara glanced at the clock on her Blackberry. Maybe Tiffani would hook up with someone else at the party tonight. Maybe *she* would hook up with someone.

MaraNara: <what are you up to tonight?>
Priceless: <mike and I are staying in.>
MaraNara: <a quiet night at home. I could do that if I had someone to be quiet with.>
Priceless: <poor mara. stuck on a free cruise, forced to go to parties, and dinners, and exotic tours.>
MaraNara: <speaking of which, I gotta go get ready for the party.>
Priceless: <ok. ttyt>
MaraNara: <bye.>

Mara stashed her Blackberry and picked up the crumpled napkin from the floor at her feet. She gave it one last crushing squeeze and tossed it in the waste basket next to the couch. The Lido lounge was one place she'd be steering clear of tonight.

One final swipe of mascara and she was done. Mara blinked twice and checked her touch up in the ladies' room mirror. The party organizers had just announced that they were going to do a version of speed dating to break the ice and get people mixing. Considering the number of potentially available attractive men she'd scouted out in the few minutes since she'd arrived, it couldn't hurt to be at her best. She stepped back and smoothed the skirt of her ubiquitous little black dress. With her dark hair and fair skin, she looked good in black.

"Hey!" Tiffani called when she returned to the lounge. "I wondered where you'd gotten to."

"Pit stop."

"Isn't this fun?"

Mara watched a couple of buff guys in cruise uniforms move the tables placed along the walls to the middle of the room. "Yeah." Watching virile young men in physical activity never failed to entertain her.

"I've never done speed dating before."

"Me neither."

The two guys made sure the candle on each of the tables was lit.

"Okay, everyone," the party MC shouted into a microphone. "Let's line up, chicks on my right." He motioned to one side of the room. "And dudes on my left."

Mara watched several people leave the lounge. Where had they found this guy? If she didn't have to write a review of the party, she'd be joining the exodus.

"Come on." Tiffani grabbed her elbow and pulled her over into line.

The lights dimmed and the hunky crew men began escorting the women to the tables. Tiffani fairly bounced with excitement. "This is so fun. Do you think Alex may come after all?" she asked.

Mara scanned the line ahead and behind her. The

old Alex would have been in his glory with all these women. That Alex never missed a party or an opportunity to flirt with women—plain or beautiful—except her. The Alex who had dinner with them tonight. Who knew?

"Probably not. He said he wasn't interested."

Tiffani drew her mouth into a pouty moue. "I thought he might change his mind. You being here and being an old friend and all." Her voice trailed off.

Mara flexed her toes. Why hadn't she ditched the shoes when she changed her clothes? She really should tell the poor girl that there was nothing between her and Alex. There never had been, except for the old childish crush she'd left behind in Harmony Hills, along with her Backstreet Boys poster and the rest of her other teen baggage.

Mara leaned to the left and peered down the lines at the lounge doorway. *Nope, no sign of Alex.* Not that she thought there would be. A small pang of disappointment belied her conviction. She turned back to catch Tiffani's little wave as she took the arm of one of the crew men to be escorted to a table.

Mara surveyed the line of men while she waited for her escort. It was shorter than the woman's line, a lot shorter. No, maybe not. A bunch of guys were milling around at the back of the room. So how was this going to work? She'd missed the details when she was in the ladies' room. Were they going to seat all the women first, then let the men pick? Not very PC.

"Miss?" The hunky dark-haired crew man who had been moving tables smiled down at her. *Oh, my.* He had dimples. She placed her hand on his proffered arm. *Hmmm, nice, muscular.* Mara glanced sideways to see if she could glimpse a ring on his left hand. What was wrong with her? This was business. She was here to critique the singles' icebreaker event. Must be Tiffani and her perpetual chatter about Alex and what fun everything was going to be.

The crew man pulled out the chair at a small round table at the far corner of the lounge.

"Thanks." She smiled at him.

He nodded and the dimples flashed again. This job had its benefits.

Mara whipped out her official GHC ratings notebook and pencil and skimmed the check-off list for personnel ratings. Nothing about heart-starting dimples. Polite and neat appearance would have to do.

"Is this seat taken?"

"Alex! How did you get in here?"

"I have my ways." He grinned and sat down across from her.

Talk about dimples. His grin put an extra tha-thump in her heartbeat. This was the Alex she knew. Not the pod person she'd had dinner with.

She leaned forward on her elbows. "Seriously, how did you get in without being signed up ahead of time?"

"Your friend Jack." His mouth hardened ever so slightly.

"My friend? I met him this evening, same as you."

"Whatever. He knows a lot about you."

Mara backed off and fiddled with her pencil. In her mind she did a fast-forward replay of the couple of days she'd spent in the corporate office training for the cruise. Jack didn't appear in any of the scenes. She would have remembered if she'd met him before.

"I thought you worked with him." Alex leaned back in his chair in a pose that would have been casual had he not had an aura of tension around him. "Jack said you're not at the resort anymore."

The last statement sounded like some kind of accusation to Mara. Since when did she have to report her job status to Alex? For that matter, when did he start caring where she was or what she was doing? That is, if he did. Her pulse was still thumping at time and a half, but now more out of irritation.

She shrugged. "Yeah, I've moved from the resort to corporate. Public relations."

Alex raised his eyebrows in question. "I thought you were in hotel management."

Warmth that had nothing to do with her irritation flowed through her. So Alex had paid some attention to what she'd been doing. Candy said they sometimes talked about her.

"Long story." She double tapped her pencil on the table. "You still haven't told me how you got in here."

"Apparently, Jack is well connected at GHC. I said I might want to attend some of the singles events and he said no problem. When I checked in here, I was on the list."

Whoa! Sounded like Jack was someone big at GHC. Maybe she should get to know him better.

"It was a lot harder getting the ticket for your table."

"What do you mean?" Alex wanted to be with her? A trill of anticipation ran through her. She certainly hadn't gotten that impression at dinner. He'd been in his usual avoid-Mara mode.

"I had to trade all my free drinks for the whole cruise to the guy in line to be your first match."

"And you did that why?" He was up to something if he'd gone so far as trading away his free drinks to be her first speed date. But what? She would *not* give into the tiny part inside her that held the hope he was finally noticing her.

"I wanted to talk with you."

His words sparked the hope despite her rational side telling her they didn't even know each other that well anymore.

He drew a small figure eight on the table with his finger tip. "I didn't have your cabin number. Didn't want to leave a message."

"O-kay." She had a few things she wanted to ask him too.

"Hey, everyone," the party MC shouted above the increasing din. "Some of you have gotten a head start. But now, it's time to officially begin. When you hear the gong . . ." The MC paused while one of the crew men rang the large copper instrument in the middle of the stage. The sound reverberated throughout the lounge. "You have five minutes to get to know your current partner. Hear the gong again and gentlemen move on to the lady to your right." He wiggled his eyebrows. "If you connect, you can hook up after the speed dating is done. Now, let's . . . get . . . started."

The gong rang again. Mara rubbed her temples.

"You okay?"

"Yeah, that gong is getting old fast. But we're wasting time. Do you want to go first? What do you want to know? Where Candy and I hid the journal you did for senior English? Interesting stuff."

Alex leaned forward and cleared his throat. "I need a favor." His voice was low and intimate.

Intriguing. And a little disconcerting to have all that male attention suddenly focused on her. Mara tapped her foot under the table and waited.

"It's, ah, Tiffani."

He wanted her help with Tiffani? So much for that little hope. Not that she'd expected her and Alex to ever make a connection.

"She reminds me of my ex-fiancé."

Mara's heart sank further. "Really." She couldn't keep the sarcasm out of her voice.

"Yeah, except nicer."

From what Candy had said, Attila the Hun was nicer than his ex. "You said it, not me."

His forehead wrinkled in question.

She shrugged.

"I need help avoiding Tiffani. Everywhere I turn, she's there. I can't take it, not for five days straight."

"Poor baby," she murmured. "I thought all the Price brothers were used to women falling at their feet."

"Well, yeah." He flashed her a heart-stopping grin. "But, I'm out of practice. I haven't been in circulation for a while."

This was sounding more intriguing than his old journal, most of which she and Candy had figured had to have been made up. "So, what do you want me to do?"

He looked down at his hands and tapped his index finger on the table. "I thought you could—"

"Bong!"

"Time to move on, gentlemen," the MC boomed.

Alex shot him a dirty look. "Come on." He grabbed her hand.

"Wait, I can't leave."

"Why not?"

Work, that's why not. She slid her journal off the table onto her lap. "Ah, things are about to get fun."

"Without me?"

His tone was light, but he gazed at her so intently, she had to look away. She fumbled with the notebook on her lap. No one on the cruise was supposed to know what she was doing.

"I kind of promised Tiffani. We came together." That wasn't exactly a lie. They had come together.

An irritated look she remembered well flashed across

his face and then was gone. "Can we meet up later and finish talking?"

"Sure, but you're not going to stand up the woman at the next table are you?"

"Me, stand up a pretty lady? Never. I'm not actually playing. I only paid the guy for a turn with you. See?" He pointed to a man taking a seat at the next table. "There he is."

"Come on guys, move it." The MC looked directly at Alex. "We have lots more women for you to meet this evening."

"Later, by the bar?" Alex asked.

She nodded and watched him cross the room with that easy fluid gait of his until his progress was blocked by the arrival of her next speed date.

"A draft, please," Alex said to the bartender. While he waited, he watched the speed daters. It was so superficial. Like his engagement, his whole relationship with Laura. She was hotter than hot. All of his friends thought so. He'd taken the challenge and staked his claim. Done something neither of his brothers had done first—gotten engaged—and had nothing to show for it.

The bartender slid the draft across the bar. Alex paid him and raised the glass in a silent toast to Price family competition and any poor devil here—male or female— with hopes of getting something meaningful out of tonight's speed dating.

He walked to a circle of chairs around a small low

table at the end of the bar furthest away from most of the speed dating tables—but unfortunately not all of them. Tiffani tipped her head around her speed dating partner and waved. She seriously was everywhere he was. She'd probably be in his dreams tonight—and not in a good way.

He repositioned one of the chairs so that Tiffani was behind his shoulder and Mara was in his line of view. But not so that she would see him watching her. He settled back, took a sip of his drink, and enjoyed the view. Mara had her back to him. Her new short haircut showed off the graceful line of her neck. He followed that line down to the black lacing that crisscrossed the open *V* back of her black dress.

She was looking really fine. For speed dating? That didn't sound like the Mara he knew. Or did he know her? She hadn't given him any good reason for not ditching the game. He raised his glass to his lips. But this was a grown-up Mara who didn't owe him any explanations, not the teenybopper who would have come to him at the snap of his fingers. The problem was he'd kind of liked the teenybopper Mara and his long-hidden attraction to the slightly older Mara had hit him full force tonight. He took a long draw of his beer. Maybe he should take his drink back to his cabin. He lowered the glass. Or, sit here and watch the grown-up Mara.

She gestured to her speed dating partner. Nothing new there. Mara had always talked with her hands. The man facing her was tall—tall enough that Alex could see him clearly over Mara's head. He looked smooth, too smooth. Kind of like a young Jack. What had his sister Candy told him? Something about Mara always hooking up with the wrong guy. Later, he'd warn Mara off him. He took another sip. Yeah, it would be the friendly thing to do.

"Okay, that last gong wraps things up," the MC said. You're on your own now."

Alex checked his watch. An hour had passed. Seemed a lot longer. When he looked up, Mara's seat was empty. He hoped he didn't miss her in the crowd closing in on the bar. He should have told her to meet him outside.

"Hey." Mara waved to him from behind a couple who had obviously made a connection. She made her way over to him. "I almost missed you hiding over here by yourself."

Alex unfolded himself from the chair and stood to greet her. As intriguing as the back lacing on Mara's dress was, the full effect of Mara in the dress standing in front of him was something else. He leisurely took in the complete picture, right down to her bare feet.

"Lose something?" He wasn't the least bit surprised she was shoeless. He wasn't sure he'd ever seen her *in* shoes until she was a teenager.

She laughed, her blue eyes sparkling in the dim light. "Nope, I've got them right here. She lifted her right hand from behind her back. A pair of strappy shoes dangled from her pointer finger. "I couldn't take them a minute longer."

"Let's go out on the deck where we can talk." He grabbed her other hand and weaved their way through the people. Once outside, he kept her hand in his while he scouted out two vacant deck chairs. "Over there." He pointed with his other hand.

She laughed. " 'Let's go.' 'Over there.' Okay, big brother, who do you think I am, Candy?"

Alex started. Did he really sound like that? Well, yes, T.J., Jace, and he sometimes did sound domineering when they were talking to Candy. But only because they were looking out for their little sister. Mara wasn't his little sister, something he was eminently glad of at the moment. He gazed at her out of the corner of his eye. Nope. He wasn't feeling brotherly at all.

"Sorry. Would you like to sit over there?" He gestured elegantly to the vacant seats.

"Come on." She tugged him toward the chairs.

He gripped her hand tighter. It felt nice in his— small, warm, friendly.

Alex released her hand when they reached the other side of the deck. While Mara sat down, he stared over the railing. The night was still and inky black except for a smattering of stars and the 300 lights behind him blazoning the ship's outside walls.

He slid into the chair to her right and thought about pushing the chair on her other side down the deck a ways to discourage anyone from joining them.

"So," she said. "What's up that you had to pay for my undivided attention?"

He cringed. "That makes me sound skeezy."

"No more so than most guys."

"Whoa, I'm not going there." He lifted his hands in surrender.

"Good. Now, you wanted to ask me . . . ?"

"Yeah, like I said. Tiffani is everywhere I turn. So far, I'm not doing great at discouraging her. And this is only the first night of the cruise."

"Ah, the trials and tribulations of being irresistible."

"What can I say? But, seriously, I was . . . I thought maybe you could . . ."

She tilted her head to one side. Here on the far side of the deck, the ship's lights were softer, making Mara's fair complexion almost pearlescent. *Gorgeous.* What was he thinking? Easy. If Mara wasn't Mara he'd be working on getting her back to his cabin.

"Out with it," she demanded.

He breathed deeply. *Why not.* "Could you pretend to be with me whenever she's around?" *Or maybe not pretend.* He hoped she didn't read that thought in his expression.

Mara stared expressionless for a moment before she broke into laughter. "You." She stopped to catch her breath. "Want me to pretend that we're all of a sudden a couple?"

"It's not *that* funny."

"Admit it. Arranging for an attractive, interested woman to see you with another woman is totally out of character for you. Trying to hide the fact that you're with another woman is more like the Alex I know."

His chest constricted until it was almost painful to breathe. That's how Mara saw him? No way. He wasn't that bad. At least not since before he was engaged. "Then you don't know me."

"Hey, you don't have to get bent out of shape."

"Forget it. I took the cruise to relax and get away from people. It was a stupid idea. I'll just spend my time in my cabin."

Mara gave him the look. The one she reserved for him and his brothers when they did something too stupid for words.

That was about as uncool as you could get. He sounded like a spoiled fourteen-year-old.

Mara reached over and placed her hand on his arm to stop him from getting up from the chair.

"What's going on?"

He gauged her sincerity. Mara could have a sharp tongue and he didn't need any smart-ass comments. "Can you keep this to yourself? I don't need you and Candy dissecting me later in IMs."

"Moi?"

Hiding in his room might be the better option.

She patted his arm. "Sure, I can keep whatever you say between us. Sounds serious."

He shrugged. "When Laura broke our engagement, I was mad, insulted, but not that hurt. And everyone's been sympathetic, too sympathetic. They won't leave me alone. Keep wanting me to get out, circulate, not sit home."

"You never were one to sit home before."

"Granted. But I need some down time to work out some stuff, not just Laura ditching me. That's why I came on the cruise."

"And Tiffani glommed on to you at first sight."

"You got it."

"What do you want me to do?"

Mara's hand was warm on his forearm. "Holding hands is good. Or anything else." Why did he say that? He waggled his eyebrows so she would think he was kidding.

She laughed and he breathed a silent sigh of relief. He had to get himself under control.

"You want me to walk around the ship holding hands with you?" she asked.

"Stuff like that when Tiffani is around, like at the evening dinners."

"And, say, Tiffani sees me with another guy when you're not around?"

"Hadn't thought of that."

If looks could kill, Mara's would have made him the star of another TV news segment on people murdered at sea.

"Sorry." Again. What was with him? He'd never had trouble talking with Mara without insulting her before—unless he'd been teasing and insulting her on purpose.

"It's okay. I didn't come on the cruise to meet men. I've sworn off them for a while."

Interesting. He wouldn't mind knowing what that

was about. And hadn't she been sending him mixed signals of interest?

"Don't ask," Mara said.

His expression must have given him away.

"Hey." Drew, the bridegroom from dinner, slid into the vacant chair. "Hope I'm not interrupting."

Yeah, you are. Big time. A little late to ask, thanks. "Where's your wife?" Alex asked.

"All worn out," Drew answered with a slimy grin. He leaned on Mara's arm rest. "How about that drink?"

Alex shot her a look.

"No, thanks." She slid her hand down Alex's arm and twined her fingers in his.

"We're going to call it a night," Alex said.

Drew pushed himself out of the chair and gave Mara a leering smile that Alex itched to wipe off his face.

"Later," Drew said before he sauntered off.

Not if Alex could help it, although he supposed he'd have to put up with him at dinner.

His gaze caught Mara's. From her expression, she wasn't any more impressed by Drew than he was.

"Okay," she said, "I'll help you out. For a favor in return."

Chapter Four

"**A**re you propositioning me?" He leaned toward her, his voice deep and low.

"In your dreams." *And mine. My teen fantasies, at least.*

Disappointment flickered in his eyes. Or was that wishful thinking on her part?

Get a grip, Riley. Your goal is to avoid doomed relationships. The only lasting relationship Alex has ever had was with his fiancé and you are so not like her.

"I'm kidding," he said.

But maybe not totally, if his heated gaze was any indication.

"What do you have in mind?" he asked, all business again.

So much for thinking the grown-up Mara could interest him. She waited a heartbeat to regain her equilibrium. Let him squirm—just a bit—like he'd done to her.

"I figure you owe me for all the teasing and pranks you pulled on me over the years," she said.

"I wasn't that bad."

She nodded. "You were that bad."

"You were no angel yourself."

"True," she admitted, thinking back at some of the bratty things she and Candy had done to her brothers. "Hey, remember the time I accidentally locked us in the hall closet?"

Alex squirmed in his seat. "Yeah." He drew the word out to three syllables. "Why? You don't want to lock us in a closet, do you?"

That wasn't the plan, but it could be fun. And it would take care of Alex's problem with Tiffani.

It might have been the moonlight, but Alex's complexion had taken on a greenish cast.

"Still claustrophobic?" She waited for his comeback zing.

He studied the deck floor. "I've been working on it."

Mara pushed a wisp of hair off her forehead. "That was an accident. I had no idea you'd freak like that. It wasn't even dark. You'd turned the light on."

His gaze drilled into hers. "I did not freak."

"You freaked."

He folded his arms across his chest. "What seventeen-year-old boy wouldn't freak being shut in a confined space with thirteen-year-old you?"

"I was pretty obnoxious," she admitted. *And totally and absolutely Alex-crazy.* Any fears he might have had about what she might have tried locked in a closet with him would have been well founded.

"Besides, you were the one who spent the next fifteen minutes pounding on the door and shouting for someone to open it," he said.

This was more like it. She'd forgotten how much she'd enjoyed their squabbles. "I didn't know what else to do. You got all quiet and strange, not at all like yourself." And, with wisdom no one would have believed she could exercise, she'd decided she should *not* throw her arms around him and kiss him. "Actually, kind of like this evening at dinner."

"I had things on my mind." Alex clenched his fingers into fists.

"In the closet?" she teased. "What kind of things?" Maybe her restraint hadn't been so wise.

He didn't even crack a hint of a smile. "No, at dinner. So what's your favor?"

Okay, then, back to business. "I'll run interference for you with Tiffani if you'll be my guy gauge."

He raised his eyebrows. "What am I measuring?"

Mara toed a small pebble on the deck with her bare

foot. "Er, I have a bad knack for hooking up with the wrong men. Players who are married, engaged, or otherwise taken."

Alex's expression said a thousand words, none of them good.

"Not on purpose." Alex should know her better than that. "The creeps let me think they're available. I find out later that they are *not* single . . . in some potentially embarrassing situation . . . like at work or in front of all of my friends."

He unfolded his arms and placed his palms on his thighs. "For real? You have no clue?"

"No clue."

"You're not a stupid woman."

"You noticed."

He grinned. "You want me to screen men for you."

"It's not funny."

"Yes, it is."

"Come on, you're practically a pro. You've been screening men for Candy for years, you and T.J. and Jace." And now that she thought about it, they hadn't done a great job. Candy's descriptions of the dates her brothers set up for her were legendary at Uncommon Grounds, where they'd hung out between college classes.

"Not that she appreciated it." He sounded almost hurt.

"Sure, she did. The thought, at least. The men, no. Does Candy strike you as the corporate-lawyer type?"

"What's wrong with corporate lawyers?"

Mara tried hard but couldn't keep her mirth from spilling over. "You have to ask? At dinner, you were arguing the case for family law versus corporate law."

He shrugged. "But I can guarantee that none of the men we introduced to Candy were married, engaged, or otherwise involved."

"Okay. I'm convinced. You're my man."

"Even if I'm a corporate lawyer for the most part?"

"As long as you don't screen any corporate lawyers through. I can't give my mother that satisfaction."

Alex tilted his head in question.

"You know. Her life ambition."

"Come on. She's not still after you to marry a doctor or a lawyer?"

"No, she's kind of relented since Kate married a surgeon. Mother's decided my marrying a lawyer would be the perfect family balance."

"How do you stand it?"

"Her trying to direct my life? Maybe you've noticed. I run away as far and as fast as I can."

"Seriously?"

"Seriously. You might remember, that I left for college more than ten years ago and haven't been back."

"You should sit down and talk with her."

"Like that would work."

"Have you tried?"

"Only a million times." She shook her head. "You can't understand. You have different family dynamics."

"Different, but not *totally* different. Everyone has family expectations."

How could Alex even begin to compare his supportive close-knit family with her dysfunctional one?

"Yeah, but there are family expectations, and then there are 'do it or I'll disown you' expectations."

Her old longing to have a family more like Alex's surfaced. She quickly reburied it.

"Let's get back on topic." *Before I go blathering on more about my family.*

"All right. The screening. No lawyers. That knocks out Jack." A satisfied smile spread across his face.

"You thought I might be interested in Jack?"

"He sure had your attention at dinner."

"Maybe if other people had been friendlier, I would have talked to them too."

Alex had the good grace to look repentant.

"Moving on. How about Drew?" she asked.

He scowled. "Obviously taken. You weren't—"

"Excuse me?"

"Sorry, but why mention him?"

Mara hesitated. "He asked me out for drinks."

"Yeah, I kind of caught that." Alex gave her a quick once over.

She shivered under his perusal, and it had nothing to do with the light breeze off the ocean.

"You *do* attract them, don't you?" he asked.

Their gazes met and warm rage replaced the coolness. "You don't have to help me."

He averted his eyes. "Oh, I think I do."

"Hey, guys."

Mara looked over her shoulder and Tiffani waved to her. She bopped over and moved the empty chair next to Mara away from the rail, so she could face Mara and Alex. "I wondered where you all had gotten to."

Alex's gaze darted back and forth between Tiffani and the small space between their chairs, obviously calculating whether he could slip away to freedom.

Mara placed her hand on top of his and felt his muscles relax. Relief flooded his face.

"So did you meet anyone interesting speed dating?" Tiffani asked.

Alex arched an eyebrow and pinned Mara with his gaze. "Yeah, did you meet anyone interesting?"

What was he up to? She was supposed to be running interference for him. Tiffani wouldn't believe they were together if she started talking up her speed dates.

"No, not really," Mara said.

"None?" Alex asked, flipping his hand over to twine his fingers with hers in a possessive grasp.

"Well, I sure did," Tiffani said.

Alex started rubbing Mara's thumb with his. She shifted in her seat. *Okay, Alex, you can turn it down. She's met some other men.*

"A professional surfer," Tiffani continued.

That could be a match made in heaven. Mara arched her thumb over and stopped his.

"And an architect and an airline pilot. I thought that was funny, an airline pilot on a ship?"

Mara coughed to cover the snort that escaped at the girl's inanity.

"They sound interesting," Alex said.

"I'm going to meet up with the surfer dude tomorrow afternoon for a lesson in the wave pool."

I knew it. She squeezed Alex's hand. He squeezed hers back, dispelling her building impatience with Tiffani's chatter.

"That should be fun," Mara said. "You said at dinner that you're a beach person."

"Well, yeah, but Jack and you did make skiing sound worth a try. I ran into him outside the lounge. Guess he was looking for someone. Is that where you two hooked up?"

Mara tried to sort out Tiffani's conversation thread. "He—"

"I—"

Alex and Mara exchanged a quick glance. His eyes narrowed in warning.

"I was at the Promenade bar and Mara spotted me on her way out."

"So, they let you in the lounge even though you aren't signed up. Bet you could have joined the speed dating."

"No, not my thing." He looked at his watch. "Want me to walk you to your room?" Alex directed the question at Mara.

"It's still early," Tiffani piped in. "But, you're right. I have an early start tomorrow. Did I tell you that one of the crewmen invited me on a morning tour of the engine room?"

Alex froze mid-push from his seat. "Say what?"

Mara warmed at his concern. Always the big brother. He might think Tiffani a pain, but that didn't stop him from feeling protective.

"Oh, yeah," she said to reassure him that Tiffani wasn't getting herself into a dangerous situation. "I saw that tour in the itinerary we got when we boarded."

Alex finished rising in a smooth fluid motion. Mara and Tiffani joined him.

"I'll walk you back," Alex said. "Where are your cabins?"

"I'm on Riviera," Mara answered.

"Serenity deck," Tiffani said. "Star . . . starboard corner. That's what the crewman said."

She'd told the crewman where her cabin was? Tiffani needed a keeper. But it wasn't going to be him, Alex vowed to himself.

He glanced sidewise at Mara. She was shaking her head. Not at Tiffani. At him.

"Let's go."

He wasn't being that overprotective, was he?

Mara grinned.

He was. Tiffani had told him where her room was

too. How was that any different then telling the crewman? It *was* time for him to turn in.

"Who's first?" Mara asked.

"Tiffani's closest," he answered, fingers crossed that Tiffani didn't know and Mara wouldn't correct him. Mara's cabin was probably closer. Tiffani's was only a few doors up the deck from his, not that he was going to share that information with her—or Mara.

"Okay," Mara linked her arm with his and Tiffani followed suit.

Alex thoroughly enjoyed the admiring looks he got from some of the men as he walked up the deck with two beautiful women on his arms.

"Hey." Tiffani pointed as they approached the lounge. "There's Jack. Still waiting. I wonder if he got stood up. Must be hard being alone at his age."

"Jack's not that old," Mara said.

Old enough. Alex looked over at her. She couldn't be attracted to him. But they *had* talked a lot at dinner. *Nah.*

"What do you think, Alex, maybe forty five?"

Alex eyed the man leaning against the wall outside the lounge, arms crossed, ogling the woman walking by. *What I think is that the man is a first class jerk.*

He shrugged. "Forty-something. Your mother's age."

Mara's mother was younger than most of her friends' parents, young to have a twenty-eight-year-old daughter.

Their eyes met and Mara burst out laughing. "That would be perfect."

"Her very own attorney," Alex said.

Tiffani wrinkled her nose. "What are you talking about?"

Mara choked back another laugh. "Nothing."

"You had to have been there," Alex added.

"Humph." Tiffani dismissed them, walking ahead to where Jack stood. "Hi, again. Want to join us? We're walking each other back to our cabins."

Alex and Mara stopped, forming a small circle with Tiffani and Jack. He pushed from the wall. "Mara's cabin is on the Riviera deck," Jack said.

Mara had told Jack where her cabin was? She couldn't be as clueless and trusting as Tiffani. Or was he over-reacting? If so, it was his brothers' fault. They'd trained him to watch over their sister when they left for college. Now he had a tendency to step in and protect any woman he knew.

"I'm on Riviera too," Jack said, leering at Mara.

Alex tightened his arm around hers. Well, not exactly leering, but his smile was awfully friendly.

"I could walk you back," Jack continued, "and Tiffani could walk with Alex if they'd like."

Tiffani looped her arm back through his. Of course, she'd like.

Mara patted the smooth plain of her stomach. "No, after my dinner, I could use the walk."

Yes! Alex released the breath he hadn't realized he'd been holding.

She offered her other arm to Jack. "Let's all go together. Tiffani first. She's closest. Then, Jack and me."

"That sounds like a plan," Alex agreed. As soon as he had a chance, he'd reciprocate Mara's help and warn her off Jack, in case she was interested.

Tiffani's lower lip slid forward in a slight pout. "Alex, you didn't say where your cabin is."

"Nope, I didn't." He wasn't as quick to share personal information as some other people.

Tiffani kept her arm tightly linked with his and chattered all the way to her room, recapping her speed dating and plans for tomorrow.

"And what are you doing tomorrow?" she asked Jack as they reached her door.

"I have a seminar in the morning and I'm meeting some business associates for lunch."

"Too bad. I'm trying to get a bunch of us together for lunch. Right, Alex?" She beamed at him.

He didn't remember anything about lunch.

"Maybe another time," Jack said in a purely polite tone.

"You guys?" Tiffani asked.

"We'll let you know," Alex answered for him and Mara.

"Okay. Goodnight," she said, less bubbly than usual. She fiddled with the lock longer than seemed necessary, then turned and rose on her toes to give Alex a quick peck on his cheek before slipping inside.

His first reaction was to wipe his cheek. Certain Jack was watching him, he resisted and flashed a triumphant smile in Jack and Mara's direction. Let Jack think he was interested in Tiffani *and* Mara.

"Where to next?" Mara asked.

"Your cabin," he said too quickly, drawing a knowing look from Jack.

Jack could believe whatever he wanted. As unreasonable as it might be, Alex didn't like the idea of Mara alone in the dimly lit hallway with Jack.

"I want to check something out with Jack," Alex said, hoping that didn't sound lame. "Lawyer stuff."

Mara wrinkled her nose and slowed her pace. "Here's my cabin."

"See you tomorrow," Alex said as she turned to go in.

Mara stopped. She looked at him questioningly.

"Our plans," he prompted, staking his territory. Now he did sound lame.

"Yeah, sure, our plans." She stood with the door half open.

They hadn't made any plans. He knew it, Mara knew it and, from the question in her voice, now Jack knew it too.

Alex took Mara's free hand and leaned down and brushed his lips against hers. Her lips were soft, pliant, and oh so sweet. He tugged her a step closer and brushed her lips again.

Footsteps down the hall broke the silence that echoed around them. He stepped back, disengaging his finger from the laces. What was he doing? This was Mara. Little Mara. She touched two fingers to her lips and he wanted nothing more than to taste them again. Not-so-little Mara.

Her eyes cleared and she looked over at Jack, who raised an eyebrow in response.

Alex couldn't stop the grin that spread across his face when Mara turned back to him.

"Men." She shook her head at them, but a hint of a smile tugged at the corner of her mouth. Her luscious, inviting mouth. Why hadn't he noticed it before. Wait. He had back in college, when she was still in high school, and had run like hell away from its draw.

"Goodnight," she said to Jack. Her gaze softened as it settled back on Alex for a moment. "I'll see *you* tomorrow."

"Rrright. Tomorrow," he stuttered.

She turned to reopen the door and he whistled silently at the pleasing fit of her dress. He hated to see her step inside.

"You don't want to talk business," Jack said.

Alex stopped staring at the closed door like a love struck adolescent. "No." He fell into step with Jack. "You're wasting your time with Mara."

"Is that what that little show was about?"

Jack's coolness irritated him. "I know Mara. We're old friends. She doesn't date lawyers."

"Why the mini-seduction, then? My benefit? If Mara doesn't date lawyers, you're out of the running too."

Jack's taunt and challenge pricked a part of Alex that he thought he'd buried. The part that would willingly pursue Mara simply for the sake of the pursuit and prize of winning. He shook it off. "Like I said we're friends. Old friends."

"Sure you are." With that, Jack turned sharply and slid his key in to the double doors of what had to be a deluxe suite.

Alex strode away and up the escalator two steps at a time. Jack rubbed him wrong. Way wrong. Not only because of his veiled taunts about Mara. So he cared about her. So what? She was like his surrogate little sister. Sort of. Jack's smoothness raised all kinds of alarms in him. Tomorrow he'd warn Mara off Jack in no uncertain terms.

When he reached the Serenity deck, he paused at the escalator landing and peered around the corner to make sure Tiffani wasn't in the hall for some reason. The last thing he wanted was for her to know that his cabin was only doors away from hers. He gave an older couple walking by a sheepish smile and they stepped right in unison as far from him as possible. What had happened to his plan to take a nice peaceful cruise to get away from it all? *Tiffani and Mara. That's what.*

With the door shut firmly behind her, Mara plopped on the bed and dug her Blackberry and notebook out of her bag. She checked her WiFi. It wasn't picking up the wireless hot spot to connect to the Internet. But she could read the email she'd collected earlier. No sense using the limited minutes GHC was paying for to sort through her junk mail.

Spam. Spam. Spam. She clicked through and deleted the long list of unwanted offers until she saw an email address she recognized. Mother's weekly missive. Mara scrolled through. Questions about the cruise and whether she'd met any men. A comment about how Mom had always wanted to take a cruise that hinted Mara and her sister Katie might want to buy her a cruise ticket for her birthday.

Mara mentally calculated how much that might cost with her GHC discount. It might be worth it if her mother met her own doctor or lawyer onboard. A picture of Alex and Jack facing off about walking her to her cabin popped into her mind. She smiled. Nothing wrong with two eligible men, for a change, showing an interest, even if their posturing had been a little on the Neanderthal side.

Mara slid out the keyboard to type a reply. Should she mention Alex and Jack and make her mother happy? A shudder ran through her. No, that would only encourage her. Alex may have had the right idea. Fix Mom up with Jack. Why hadn't she thought of that before? She piled the pillows up behind her and leaned back. That plan would require inviting Mom down to North Carolina, including transportation, and having somewhere for her to stay. Mara was still in the dorms at the resort. Finding an apartment in Asheville was her number one priority when the cruise was done.

Of course, any apartment Mara could afford wouldn't measure up to her mother's standards. It would be too much like the apartments Mara and her sister grew up in. No, Mother would have to stay at the resort and no way could Mara afford that, unless Kate would kick in. Then, too, she'd have to find out where Jack worked at GHC, so she could get him and her mother together. She let her head drop back to the pillows and rolled it back and forth. She'd never pull it off. But a woman could dream, couldn't she?

As she considered how to reply innocuously to her mother's email and free herself for another week, Mara's thoughts drifted to Alex. She was looking forward to "protecting" him from Tiffani too much, way too much. She hopped off the bed and pulled her report forms from the bedside table. Settling back in the pillows, she nibbled the top of her pen. What had happened to her plan to swear off men and concentrate on her career?

Chapter Five

Alex paced the deck in front of the fitness center, stopping at each turn to survey its length and check his watch. The class should have been out three minutes ago. He grabbed Mara's arm as soon as she stepped out of the center. A flash of hot pink at the far end of the deck sent prickles up his spine.

"In here, quick." Alex pulled Mara toward the open door of a supply closet.

"What are you doing?"

"Tiffani. She's headed this way. I spent two long hours with her this morning while you were checking out the women's kickboxing class."

"That class was way cool. Best cardio ever, and I'm totally ready to defend myself against anything."

He pulled her into the closet with him and his heart sank when he heard the door click shut behind her.

"Why did you do that?" he asked.

"What? You're the one who dragged me in here."

"The door." He struggled to keep his breathing modulated by telling himself it was because Mara was standing so close to him, not because the walls were closing in. He had totally mastered his claustrophobia with subliminal relaxation CDs before he'd come on the cruise. In fact, he'd brought them with him for a refresher if his cabin started feeling too cramped.

"Oh." Her voice went soft. "The strap on my bag caught the door knob. I'll open it."

He waited while she turned the knob. *Deep breaths like the CDs said. That's it. We'll be out of here in a minute.* Sweat beaded on his brow. It was an awfully long minute.

"Alex? I can't open it. I think it's locked."

"Let me try." He reached for the door knob and collided with her, which diverted his mind from the oppressive darkness of the increasingly smaller-feeling closet. He changed direction and reached for the knob with his other hand at the same time Mara stepped away from him. They bumped again.

"Sorry." She inched away.

He grabbed the door knob and twisted it like his life depended on it. It turned ninety degrees and stopped. He twisted it harder. It didn't move. "Damn. Who locks a closet from the inside?" he muttered.

"Are you okay?" Mara's voice sounded far away, although he could feel her heat right beside him.

"It won't open." That was brilliant, but with the lack of oxygen to his brain what could he expect? Alex tried to lengthen his short shallow breathing as he'd trained himself to do. Maybe that would help slow down his racing pulse.

"We'll figure something out." She rubbed his arms from elbow to shoulders.

Sweat trickled down his collar. Between her touching him and the thick darkness surrounding him, he wasn't going to last long.

He needed an anchor. He slipped his arms around her waist and hugged her to him. If he was going to suffocate to death, he might as well enjoy himself doing it.

"I lied." She murmured against his shirt front. "I'm not sorry."

"Sorry?" His voice was a hoarse whisper.

"For locking us in."

His heart beat a rapid tattoo against his chest.

"What are y'all doing in my closet?" The words washed over Alex like ice water.

He stared dumbly at Mara. The expression on her face, which was illuminated by the back light from the now-open door, was a cross between bemusement and sheer mortification. She bit her bottom lip and his temperature shot up until he was hard pressed not to take her in his arms again.

"Are you deaf or just dumb?"

That voice. It sounded just like . . . it couldn't be . . . He looked over Mara's shoulder. "Mrs. Van Dusen?" He did a double take. The cleaning woman standing in the doorway sounded like and looked like their elementary school principal. He time-traveled back to the drably painted office of Harmony Hill Elementary School—a place he'd spent far too much time, often only because he was the last of the Price boys.

Mara's wide eyes and white-on-white face told him she was right there with him. Mara had been an imp.

She spun around, smoothing her T-shirt and running her hands over her unruly curls.

"Don'tcha have rooms? Or are you hiding?" The cleaning woman's mouth twisted in disgust.

Relief flowed through Alex. Mrs. Van Dusen would never say *don'tcha*.

"Come on." Mara pulled him out to the deck.

Alex blinked to adjust his eyes to the bright sunlight. A flush of embarrassment had added color to her cheeks.

"See," she said, "I told you we'd get out." She tapped his chest with her forefinger. "And you forgot all about being claustrophobic."

Alex didn't know whether to shake her or kiss her. He ran his gaze over her from the inviting smile on her face down to her see-through plastic flip flops and scarlet polished toenails. His thoughts ran to inviting Mara to see the view from his cabin balcony. But he wouldn't. She deserved better. He shook his head in wonder at his re-luctance. Normally, that would have been a sure move for him. When had being chummy to ward off Tiffani turned into these kind of real, protective feelings for Mara?

"Hey, you guys."

Alex turned to see Tiffani bearing down on them. A part of him was actually glad to see her.

"Want to get some lunch and then go swimming? I found the cutest bikini and cover up at the gift shop." Tiffani held up a bag with *Carolina* blazed across it in fancy script writing.

Mara mouthed "no" to Alex while Tiffani dug in the bag for her purchase.

"Can you believe I only brought one suit on a cruise?" She pulled out a small scrap of black fabric. "Isn't it just so me?"

Alex's temperature ticked up as he imagined Mara in the skimpy little suit. It was barely more than a couple triangles with strings.

Mara smiled at him as if she read his thoughts and his internal thermometer headed for record territory.

"They have them in all different colors. There's one in red that would look good with your coloring," Tiffani said to Mara. "Let me show you the cover up and other stuff I got." She handed Mara a filmy shirt.

He shook an image of Mara in the shirt and little swimsuit from his mind.

"So, what do you say?" Tiffani asked.

"Hmmm?" Alex replied.

"About swimming," Tiffani said. "You said we'd do something later."

He had? Didn't sound like him. He'd spent most of the morning trying to escape her, which had led to his and Mara's meeting in the closet.

"Yeah, you said you'd catch me later," she said impatiently. "I figured you wanted to get together this afternoon." She pulled a couple more pieces of clothing from the bag to show Mara. "Well?"

He sighed. Did Tiffani actually think he meant that he planned to see her later? She was as bad as Mara had been as a teen. Mara had always read more than he meant into anything nice he'd said to her. He shifted his weight from his right foot to his left. Or maybe she'd been picking up what he had really been thinking. So he'd stopped being nice.

His conscience pricked him again. What had his actions in the closet said to Mara? Was he offbase thinking she was interested too? Maybe she'd just been flirting, playing him like his fiancé had. But why? What could she gain? He pushed his hand through his hair.

Mara handed the clothes back to Tiffani and she stuffed them back into the bag. "So, what about swimming?"

"We have—" Mara started.

"Nothing better to do," Alex finished for her.

Mara glared at him. "Nothing better?" she repeated.

How could she be making him feel guilty about not trying to spirit her off somewhere to be alone?

"Oh, stop." Tiffani reprimanded them. "I know you guys are together, regardless of what you said last night. You don't have to pretend with me that you're not. If you have other plans, tell me. You're not the only people I know onboard, you know."

Great! Tiffani was loading on the guilt too. He hadn't carried this big a load of guilt since . . . since never. And what was with the pretend you're not together. He thought he and Mara had been doing a pretty good job of *being* together. Mara's annoyance was proof that he hadn't lost his touch. His gaze bounced between Tiffani and Mara. Yeah, her expression hadn't softened and neither had Tiffani's.

Mara shot him a look that could have withered a thirty-foot oak tree and looped her arm through Tiffani's. "Come on," she said. "Let's go shopping. I'd like to see that red suit. Maybe by the time we're done, Alex will have decided what he wants."

Ouch! The sting of Mara's words was only partially soothed by watching the sassy sway of her hips as she marched Tiffani down the deck.

Mara tossed the shopping bag on her bed. Tiffani had been right. The red swimsuit fit like it had been made for her. It would serve Alex Price right if she put it on and met Tiffani, her surfer dude from speed dating, and his friend at the pool. But she had no desire to do that. She'd expended her desire earlier with Alex at a cost that far exceeded the exorbitant price she'd paid for the swimsuit.

So much for all her hard-learned lessons. A little attention from Alex and she was sixteen again and inventing ways to be alone with him. No. She caught herself before she stamped her foot. She *was* acting sixteen. But it was he who pulled *her* into the closet, hung on to her like a lifeline until the cleaning woman opened the door. What was with him and the mixed signals he sent her?

Her stomach growled. Nothing like passion followed by fury to build up an appetite. Well, that and skipping lunch. She scarfed down the complemintary chocolate that housekeeping had left on the bed. Another pound of super dark chocolate or so and she might start feeling okay. She paced the small room, trying to walk off her restless energy. Too bad the kickboxing class wasn't now instead of this morning. She could really kick some butt about now. Maybe she should go to the work out room and run a few hundred miles on the treadmill.

Beep, beep, beep. The pager on her Blackberry went off. Had she forgotten a work appointment? She pushed the power button to light the screen and instant message box appeared.

Priceless: <hey.>

Mara sat on the edge of the bed.

MaraNara: <hey yourself. shouldn't you be in class?>

Priceless: <cancelled.>

MaraNara: <what's up?>

Priceless: <wedding stress. I wish you were here to help.>

MaraNara: <me too.>

Priceless: <dad and mike are trying to be helpful, but they're such men.>

MaraNara: <men are a completely different species.>

A species, which if Alex was at all typical, she didn't understand. Maybe because Mother Dearest didn't allow any male influences in her and her sister's lives until she deemed them old enough to husband hunt.

Priceless: <you've met someone!>

MaraNara: <what? you know I've sworn off men.>

Priceless: <get real.>

MaraNara: <am real.>

Priceless: <nope. you only criticize men when you're involved with one.>

Mara took a deep breath. If anyone could help her figure out Alex, it was Candy.

MaraNara: <it's alex.>

She bit her bottom lip waiting for Candy's reaction.

Priceless: <as in my brother alex?>

She rolled her eyes. How many other Alexes did Candy know on this cruise?

MaraNara: <one and the same.>
Priceless: <no kidding?>

Mara blew a stray hair out her eyes. Maybe she was wrong about Candy being helpful.

MaraNara: <no kidding.>
Priceless: <i thought he was acting weird>
MaraNara: <he was. he is.>
Priceless: <???>
MaraNara: <we got locked in a cleaning supply closet.>
Priceless: <interesting. and?>

Mara hesitated. She didn't want to creep Candy out. Alex *was* her brother. But she could really use Candy's advice. Mara tapped in her answer.

MaraNara: <we got kind of friendly.>
Priceless: <okay>

Ugh! Candy *did* think it was icky.

MaraNara: <so, this cleaning lady interrupts, we get out on the deck and he turns all cool. am i a crazy or what?>
Priceless: <no, he's–>

The instant message window suddenly closed and Mara's Blackberry screened flashed NO INTERNET CONNECTION. Mara tapped the refresh button. NO INTERNET CONNECTION.

Great! The WiFi access was listed as available only in the lounges, conference rooms, and other public areas. But she'd picked it up a couple of times in her cabin too. She tapped her foot on the floor. *That was no help.* What had Candy been about to tell her? Mara punched in her phone number. The international roaming would probably cost her a fortune, but she had to know what Candy had been about to say.

"Sorry, your call cannot be completed," a pleasant computer voice told her. A second try yielded the same results.

She fluffed the bed pillows in hopes of finding a stray chocolate. Should she try to make things right with Alex at dinner? No, she couldn't do that. Tonight was her night to have dinner with the captain. Her job put her on a list of a select few guests who were chosen at random to dine with the captain one night during the cruise.

Then again, why should *she* make things right when Alex was the one at fault. Mara went to the wardrobe to pick out something to wear. If she ran into Alex after dinner, she could act just as cool is he. *Yep.* She hugged herself, remembering the feel of Alex's arms around her in the closet. That's what she'd do, she'd act cool and detached, even if it killed her.

Chapter Six

"**H**ey, where were you last night?" Alex cut in ahead of Mara in the brunch buffet line.

"Excuse me." The man behind Mara tapped Alex on the shoulder.

"It's okay." Alex brushed the man off. "I only want to talk to her. I ate earlier."

Mara saw her chance. She grabbed her breakfast plate and escaped to the coffee bar while Alex dealt with her fellow diner. She wasn't ready to see Alex yet. She'd purposely waited for brunch to avoid running into him before she'd had her morning dose of caffeine.

"A double mocha latte, please," she said to the woman behind the coffee bar.

"Late night?"

Alex's voice startled her and the coffee slopped over

the top of the cup and ran down over her fingers. "Ouch." She shifted the cup to the other hand and shook off the hot liquid.

"Hey, sorry." He lifted her hand and kissed her knuckles. "All better?" he asked rubbing her fingers.

She winced at the fission of pain-pleasure that ran up her arm. It had nothing to do with hot coffee.

"Did I hurt you?"

She shook her head.

He took the coffee cup and directed her to a small table in an empty corner of the dining room. Placing the cup on the table, he pulled a chair out for her, then sat in the opposite seat. Once she'd settled in, he leaned forward on his elbows, his expression as serious as she'd ever seen it.

"About yesterday, I was an idiot."

"Um, yeah." She sipped her coffee waiting for a more formal apology.

"I never should have . . ." He swallowed hard enough that she could see the muscles work in his neck. "The closet. I didn't mean to . . ."

Mara gripped the coffee cup like a lifeline. He wouldn't. He couldn't be apologizing for turning to her.

"Yes." He corrected himself. "I did mean to. You're gorgeous. Who wouldn't?"

Mara's heart raced. She made herself slowly and deliberately take another sip of coffee.

"But it's not what you think," he said.

She forced the coffee down. Was this where he warned

her off? Told her not to expect anything more than an ocean fling? A chill ran through her. She set the coffee mug down. "Alex, I'm all grown up now."

"Yeah," he mumbled. "That's the problem. Any other woman and I'd—"

"Any other woman?"

A muscle worked in Alex's jaw. "Not like that."

Mara held his gaze. "Then, like what? Being Candy's friend makes me untouchable?"

"Yes . . . no." He buried his head in his hands and shook it.

Mara took a deep breath. "Maybe it's time you grew up too, and stopped the game of now I like you, now I don't you've been playing for the past ten years." She struggled to keep the tremor out of her voice and tears from her eyes.

His head shot up. He took her hand in his. "I have been doing that." He caressed her palm. "Yesterday. I, ah, didn't want you to think it was only lust."

Mara had never seen Alex look so uncertain.

"What's wrong with a little attraction?" Her voice cracked, breaking the light tone she was striving for. She tensed when Alex didn't smile in agreement.

His expression darkened. "Like you could have been any woman? I could have been any man."

She squeezed his hand.

"You're not making this easy. I wanted it to be more. Then Tiffani interrupted. You make me feel things I'm not good at dealing with. All right?"

"Things like what? Attraction? Caring?

"Yeah."

Mara sat speechless for a minute. "Yes. I'm good with that."

"Okay."

She could swear he sighed with relief.

"Are you going to eat those sausages?" He pointed at her long-forgotten breakfast plate. "Because, if not, all this deep talk has made me hungry."

That was it? Discussion over? A smile spread across her face. Alex Price had just said out loud that he had feelings for her. "Take whatever you want." She spread her arms expansively over the table.

"Alex, Mara!" He looked up to see Tiffani and her blond surfer dude, as Mara called him, bearing down on their table. What did they want? He was just getting back on Mara's good side.

"You're still having breakfast?" Tiffani asked.

He looked down at Mara's sausages, then up at Mara. She was still smiling at him. His heart did a double beat. Maybe he hadn't sounded like a total dork when he'd tried to tell her how much he liked her and asked her for her breakfast all in one sentence.

Tiffani went into her now-familiar hands-on-hips pose. "Well. We were all supposed to meet at ten to go on shore together. Jack and Christie and Drew are probably at the gangway waiting." She tapped her foot.

Mara rolled her eyes, and he choked back a laugh.

Tiffani might want to seriously look into a job as a cruise director—or a drill sergeant. "Mara got to breakfast late. I'm helping her finish up."

Mara pushed her chair back. "Don't blame this on me." She stood and tugged at his hand across the table. "I was going to catch a quick bite by myself and he . . ." She tugged harder until he stood too. "He came along and distracted me."

He distracted her? She was the distraction and a wicked one at that.

"I need to get my bag and notebook from my cabin," Mara said, "and we'll be right with you." She kept his hand firmly gripped in hers.

"All right," Tiffani relented. "See you in a couple minutes by the gangway." She and her friend headed one way. Alex and Mara went the other.

"What do you say we blow off Tiffani?" He released her hand and slid his arm around her waist. She leaned into him. Good sign.

"I can't," she softly answered.

"Why not."

"I just can't." Her voice crescendoed up.

She wasn't. He stopped walking. *She wouldn't.* He turned her toward him and rested his hands on either side of her waist. "Is this payback?"

"What?" She looked at him as if he'd grown a third eye.

If he could grow a third eye, maybe he could also fade away and join her and the others at the gangway like he'd never started this stupid conversation. He blinked. He was still here and so was Mara, looking not at all happy.

"Er." He cleared his throat. "Payback. You know, like when we were kids?"

She stared at him, her face totally devoid of expression. He did the only thing he could think of. He kissed her.

"No," she murmured against his lips.

He drew back slightly. "You want me to stop?"

"No," she repeated. "Not payback." She pulled his head toward her and brushed her lips against his.

Alex released Mara. The cool ocean breeze that filled the distance between them as they parted did come close to the chill of that grating voice. He looked over her shoulder. The Mrs. Van Dusen look-alike housekeeper frowned at them.

Not again.

Mara turned to see what he was looking at. She took his hand. "Come on." She dragged him toward her cabin.

Who was he to argue? He waited while she unlocked the door. She waved him in.

"Give me a sec to pack my bag."

"You wouldn't rather stay?" He leaned against the door and crossed his arms. "Let the others go ahead without us?"

"Can't." She tossed some clothes off the chair on to the bed. "I was sure it was here. Do you see a spiral notebook anywhere?"

"The blue one there on the floor?"

"Yep, thanks." She picked up a notebook and put it in her canvas bag. "Now, all I need is my sunglasses." She rummaged through another bag on the desk. "Got 'em." She waved the shades at him. "All set. Let's go."

"Or stay." He pushed off the door.

"The others are waiting."

"They won't miss us." He stepped toward her.

Indecision spread across her face. "I have to go. For wor—" She stopped and yanked the bag strap higher on her shoulder.

Work. She was going to say work. Something clicked in his brain. The cruise had something to do with her job.

She closed the distance between them. "I've always wanted to see St. Bart's. It's the highlight of the cruise."

Alex vaguely remembered reading those same words in the literature his ex-fiancée had given him about the cruise.

"Your choice." He opened the door for her and followed her out. They didn't have to stay with the others. A day with Mara on a Caribbean beach wasn't a bad thing. Maybe she'd bought the red version of the swimsuit Tiffani had shown them yesterday.

Alex guided Mara around the cleaning lady, who was in the hall again—or still.

"It would serve her right if I wrote her up," Mara said when they were past the woman.

"So, that's why you're on the cruise?" he asked.

"Huh?"

"You're on the cruise as part of work."

Mara looked from side to side and over her shoulder, as if making sure no one else was in hearing distance. "I don't suppose you'd believe that I meant the little GHC How Did I Do? check list on the desk in all the cabins."

"Nope." He slipped his arm around her waist.

"It's not like I don't trust you."

Warmth filled Alex, although he wasn't sure how far she *should* trust him. Or how far he trusted himself. He was on the rebound from his engagement. He could be falling in love with being in love, like he had with his fiancée.

"No one is supposed to know," Mara said. "It's part of my employment contract, so people don't give me better than usual service to get a good write-up."

She spoke so softly that he had to lean closer to hear. The tangy scent of her shampoo tickled his nose and boosted the amperage in every nerve ending in his body. His fiancée's shampoo hadn't done that.

"I'm kind of like a secret shopper." She nibbled her bottom lip.

"Cool! And what a way to start. With a free vacation," he added with overexuberance.

She wrinkled her nose at him, and he wanted to kiss the tip of it. He had to get a grip on himself.

"Yeah," she said, "but it's not all fun and games. Tomorrow, I have to go to one of the onboard seminars. I'd thought I'd said good-bye to formal classes when I left U Albany."

"Shouldn't be that bad." He squeezed her closer. "I'll go with you."

"Appreciated. But have you seen the list?"

"I didn't look. Taking a class wasn't something I'd planned on doing.

"Exactly. Maybe Jack's giving his tomorrow."

"That ought to be good. We can check it out when we get back. For now, let's go enjoy St. Bart's."

Mara admitted to herself that she'd probably enjoy anywhere if it was with Alex.

When they reached the top of the gangway, she spotted Tiffani and the others waiting at the bottom. "I'd hoped they'd left without us."

"Tiffani? Not a chance," Alex said. "Too bad we can't tell her you have to follow a certain agenda for work."

Mild panic set in. "Alex, you can't. No one is supposed to know."

"Hey." He squeezed her side. "I'm teasing. I wouldn't."

"I know. But this is my first assignment. I'm a little edgy. I don't want to screw it up."

"I'll be good." He flashed his dimples with a quick smile. "Looks like we have to sign out or something over there." He pointed to a woman with a clipboard.

"Yeah, we have to sign off and on the ship." They joined the line in front of the woman.

"Just like church camp." Alex said. "Sign on the bus, sign off the bus."

"Wait. I don't remember you going to church camp."

"Sure, the summer after freshman year. Alyssa Sanford and I were dating. She was into church youth group, so I joined and the group went to Camp Fowler for a week."

"A girl. I should have known. But I really don't remember." Of course, it predated her mad crush on Alex. That didn't strike until the next year when she was in seventh grade and he was a sophomore.

"Why *would* you remember?"

Mara shrugged. Maybe she hadn't been as obvious in her prepubescent crush on Alex as she'd thought.

"You were just a little twerp then," he teased.

"Little twerp, huh?" She reached over and poked him in a spot she knew was vulnerable, his right side just below his rib cage. She and Candy used to gang up on him and tickle him mercilessly when he picked on them. That is, if they could catch him. Taunt muscles moved under her fingertips.

"Hey!" He squirmed away. "No fair. You're not ticklish. Or you weren't ticklish."

He reached toward her, but stopped short of poking her in the ribs when the couple ahead of them moved, giving Mara a full view down the gangway. Tiffani waved up at them. She half-heartedly waved back.

The last people between them and the cruise assistant moved on.

"Hi," the assistant greeted them. "May I have your names, please?"

"Mara Riley."

The woman made a checkmark on the paper on her clipboard. "Have a nice day, Ms. Riley." She smiled at Alex.

"Alex Price."

Another check. "And here's your cabana/luncheon reservation." The GHC cruise assistant handed Alex a small card with script writing.

Wow! Alex had reserved a cabana for them? With lunch? A flutter started deep inside. The man sure knew how to grovel. She ran over her work agenda in her head. Historic tour in the morning. Snorkeling in the afternoon. She did have a couple hour breaks in between. But if he'd reserved it for the whole day . . . She hoped he hadn't paid a lot. Maybe the others could use it too.

"Cabana?" he asked dumbly.

"Yes, sir. You reserved it as part of your honeymoon package." The woman smiled over at Mara.

The cabana had been part of the package Alex and his fiancée had planned. Mara had a good idea how a punctured balloon felt. She should have known. They'd been clicking, but not on an expensive cabana-for-a-day level.

"Oh, I'd forgotten." Alex said. A sheepish blush darkened his cheeks. He nodded his thanks to the cruise assistant and they started down the gangway.

He fingered the card. "Is your whole day scheduled?"

"Pretty much."

The side of his mouth pulled up in a half-grimace.

Sympathy tugged at Mara. Alex had scheduled the

cruise as his honeymoon trip. She scanned his face for signs of delayed regret. His expression was more perturbed than disturbed.

"I hate to see the money go to waste," he said. "I should have given it back. Maybe I could have gotten a refund."

Nope, no emotional regrets. Alex's concern seemed to be strictly financial. Candy had always said he was careful with his money—and not in a good way.

"Or, at least, someone else could have used it."

They stepped onto the dock.

"Used what?" Tiffani asked. She turned to Mara. "Took you long enough, by the way."

Mara's brain went into double action for a pithy retort. But Tiffani's genuine frown at Mara not meeting her schedule told Mara it wasn't worth the effort.

"Alex reserved a cabana," she said.

"Cool!" Tiffani said.

"Why didn't you think of that?" a female voice demanded.

Mara looked over Tiffani's shoulder to see Christie and Drew approaching them, neither one of them looking too happy.

"Maybe I could have if you hadn't had to have the wedding extravaganza of the decade. We wouldn't have had to go cheap on the honeymoon."

A strange look passed over Alex's face. "Here, you guys take it." He tried to hand Christie the cabana card.

She shook her head.

"Take it," Drew hissed.

"Yeah, take it," Alex said. "We can all meet there for lunch."

"Okay." She reluctantly accepted it.

"You, too, about lunch," Alex said to Tiffani and her date.

"Sounds good. We can all hang out at the beach for the afternoon." She squeezed surfer boy's bicep. "Brad's going to give me more surfing lessons."

He smiled down at her.

Looked like Tiffani had made a connection.

"What are you guys doing this morning?" she asked.

"A history tour," Mara answered.

Tiffani crinkled her nose. "We're going shopping."

"We're going to use that cabana," Christie said.

"After I see if I can find a net café to check the market mid-morning trend. If I've pegged it right, I may be able to make a killing on a short sale," Drew said.

Christie gave him a poisonous look.

"Hey, where's Jack?" Mara asked to steer the conversation elsewhere.

"The party pooper," Tiffani said. "He told Drew and Christie that he'd decided to stay onboard and work on his seminar stuff for tomorrow."

"Okay, then. We'll see you guys later. Alex and I have a tour bus to catch."

"You know how I said Tiffani reminded me of my ex?" Alex asked. "I take that back."

"Tiffani's not bad in her own adolescent cheerleader way," Mara agreed.

"I wouldn't go that far." Alex laughed. His expression grew more serious. "Nope, the ex is more like Drew. Or was more like Drew before she met her forest ranger. Ruled by money and appearances."

"Not to hurt your feelings or anything, but no one— well, Candy and I—could figure out what you saw in her."

"I was all wrapped up in her good looks . . ."

Some questions were better left unasked. Laura was stunning. But if Mara wanted to pursue Alex, it couldn't hurt to know what had attracted him to his ex-fiancée. *Whoa, stop that thought.* Her chasing Alex days were long over.

"I didn't see how much she was lacking in character and personality." He slid his fingers through hers and squeezed her hand.

A tremble of excitement ran through her. Nope, this was different. The pursuit was mutual.

She gave him an exaggerated once over. "And you're not bad yourself."

He grinned, flashing his dimples. "Seriously, I thought Laura and I had a lot in common, wanted the same things."

"And you didn't?"

He shrugged. "More like neither of us wanted what we thought we wanted."

Well, that was cryptic. Dare she ask what he did want?

Before Mara could decide, they reached the land end of the dock. "Where are we going?" Alex asked.

Mara pulled her notebook from the pocket of her bag and flipped it open. "Right here. The tour bus is supposed to pick us up at the end of the dock."

She gazed around. Several people were milling about in a loose line near a light post. "There." She pointed.

They joined the group. Alex dropped her hand and rested his arm loosely around her shoulder. She'd save her questions about what Alex might want for later and just enjoy the day with him.

Chapter Seven

Mara headed to the cabana after her scuba-diving lesson. Alex was the only one inside.

Alex dropped a light kiss on the top of her head and whispered "missed you" in her ear. He'd changed into swim trunks and smelled of sun, salt, and sand.

She shivered. They'd only been apart a couple of hours, but she'd missed him too.

"Cold?" He wrapped a towel around her shoulders.

The opposite, actually. She hugged her arms to her chest.

"Hi." Tiffani entered the cabana, her friend trailing behind. "How was the scuba lesson?"

"Ah." Mara had trouble putting together a coherent sentence with Alex standing so near. "Great."

He stepped away, and she regained her equilibrium.

"I'd love to do some more. The fish, the coral. It was all so beautiful. I'll have to see if there are any diving schools in Charleston."

"Jack could probably tell you," Christie said as she and Drew stepped into the cabana, arms draped around each other, looking like the newlyweds they were.

The tropical sun must have improved their moods.

"Speaking of Jack," Tiffani said, "I'd swear I saw him hanging around the scuba school this afternoon when we were walking back to return the surf boards we'd rented."

Alex moved back closer to Mara. "You said he was staying back at the ship."

"That's what he told me," Christie said. "Maybe he changed his mind."

"You know, I saw someone who looked just like Jack outside the cathedral this morning," Drew added.

Mara's stomach flip-flopped. She'd thought she'd seen him there too, across the street when their tour group had come out of the cathedral. When she'd waved, the man had ducked into a shop. She shook off her unease. "You know what they say. Everyone has a double."

"I guess," Tiffani said. "But he is a little weird, hanging out with us rather than people his own age."

"Ah, Tiff," Drew said, "Jack was assigned to our dining table, and you're the one who keeps inviting him to do stuff with us."

"I'm with Tiffani," Alex said. "I don't like the guy."

"I didn't say I didn't like him. I just said he was a little weird," Tiffani protested.

"All right," Mara said to change the subject. "Are we going to stand around and talk about Jack or enjoy this beautiful beach?"

"I'm kind of beached out," Tiffani said.

"Come on," Mara coaxed. "You said you loved the beach."

"I do, but we've been surfing." Tiffani stopped and smiled at her companion. "Or trying to surf since lunch. I'm tired."

"How about you guys?" Mara asked Christie and Drew.

"We're pretty beat too," Christie said.

"Yeah, we did some sightseeing and I had to check in with a client this morning since we have regular cell phone service here. That should keep me in good with the big guys. You know how it is. Closed a big deal." Drew shot Alex a guy smile. "Then, after lunch here— thanks, man. She shopped me half to death."

Mara waited for Christie to fling virtual daggers at her husband for his last remark. Instead she smiled benevolently at him. *That must have been some shopping trip.* Apparently it had made up for his failings this morning.

"Hey, if you're going to hang out here, do you want to play some poker with us?" Tiffani asked.

"Sure," Drew said.

Christie nodded. "Do you have cards?"

"I picked up the coolest deck when we were shopping." Tiffani pulled a small box from her swim bag and held it up. "The face cards are all in island dress."

Fabulous! All she had left to do for today's work assignment was to observe fellow passengers on the beach. And everyone wanted to stay in and play poker in the cabana. She'd figured it would be a snap. They'd all go play beach volleyball or something.

"We can play six handed," Tiffani said.

"Maybe later," Alex said. "I want to get some more sun." He took Mara's elbow. "Ready?"

"Ah, yeah."

He guided her out of the cabana. "What's wrong?"

"It's work. I'm not supposed to talk about it.'

"Right, what's wrong?"

Mara breathed in the fresh salty air. She hadn't realized how close and stuffy it had been in the cabana. She released her breath. Alex already knew about her assignment. What could it hurt? She glanced around to make sure no one would overhear, then shook her head. The way she was acting, you'd think she was a spy and this was a matter of national security, rather than marketing research. She explained how she was supposed to observe cruisegoers on the beach.

"You know. What they're doing, what they're saying. I'd thought we'd all hang out and I'd observe."

"You can observe me," Alex said with a grin.

She eyed him from his sun-kissed hair to his toes curled in the white sand. Now, that's one job she wouldn't mind at all.

"I need a little more perspective than that. I'm supposed to include people, plural, that I've met on the cruise."

He grabbed her hand. "We'll walk around the beach and observe."

"How will I know if the people are from the ship or not?"

"We'll recognize some. Like the guy over there from the brunch line. And how much does it matter? I'm sure GHC wants to know whether this port of call is a place where people enjoy themselves. Will it draw people to the cruise?"

Mara waffled for a split second. "You're right."

"That's my woman."

Her heart skipped a beat at his possessive endearment.

"Write this down," he directed. "I'm a cruise goer who is thoroughly enjoying the port of call. Although it's probably the company." He squeezed her hand.

"I can't report that," she said once she'd caught her breath. If he didn't quit zinging these lines at her, she might just need an oxygen tank.

"Sure, you can. People come on cruises to meet people. Hooking up with people they like makes the cruise more enjoyable."

She shook her head. "You have an answer for everything. You always have."

He grinned and shrugged. "What can I say? I'm a lawyer."

"I'll try not to hold that against you."

"Careful, I'll tell your mother you're hanging out with lawyers."

"You wouldn't. She'd—"

"Hi." A statuesque redhead Mara recognized from the speed dating party interrupted to invite them, or, rather, Alex to join a beach volleyball game she was organizing.

"What do you say?" Alex asked.

Mara eyed the woman and her Amazon friends at the volleyball net. They'd cream her. And that was just the women. The men looked pro too. Pilates and kickboxing were more her style. "Why don't you play if you want, and I'll watch."

"We'll be right there," he said to the redhead. "Now you can observe me *and* other people from the ship."

"Yeah, yeah." They walked over to the net. Mara spread a towel from her bag while Alex pulled off his shirt and flexed his muscles. "Show-off."

He wrinkled his forehead. "What? I said I wanted to get some more sun."

She sat crossed-legged on the towel and waved him off. "Go play." She opened her notebook and took the cap off her pen, but the *wham* of the first serve distracted her.

Alex raced forward and set up the ball. The man could really move. Amazon redhead spiked it over the net for the first point. Mara watched Alex rotate into place to serve. With perfect timing, he tossed the ball with his left hand and raised his right. *Slam!* Point two. The other team couldn't even get under his serve to attempt a return. Mara recapped her pen and set it and her notebook aside to watch.

When the game set ended, Alex trotted over to her, his teammates congratulating him on scoring the final winning point. "Short set," he said. "Did you get enough to start your report?"

Mara's gaze fixated on the beads of sweat glistening in the dusting of hair on his chest. "Huh?"

"Your observations." He pointed at her closed notebook.

"No, ah." She felt her cheeks pinking. "The game was too exciting. I'll jot the stuff down now that it's over." She fumbled with her pen.

"Whew! I'm hot," he said.

She couldn't argue with that.

"Want to take a quick dip?"

"No, you go ahead. I want to get my notes down."

She opened her notebook and began writing some of the comments about the beach and cruise she'd heard during the game. An eerie feeling of being watched came over her. Mara glanced around but didn't see anything out of the ordinary. Most of the volleyball players had headed over to the tiki bar.

"Do you have another towel?" he asked.

"No, but you can have this one." She stood, shook the towel out, and handed it to him.

He rubbed his head and ran the towel over his chest.

"Hey, can you get my back?" He handed her the towel and turned around.

She allowed herself a moment to admire the width of his shoulders before she started to dry the drops of saltwater that glistened on his smooth, tanned skin.

"Looks like you have an admirer," he said pointing toward a distant overlook.

The movement of his muscles beneath her touch rippled through her like the soft waves of the sea on the shore. She followed the line of his arm and saw a man with binoculars. He somehow looked familiar. The weird feeling she'd had earlier replaced the pleasant ripple.

Mara tried to laugh it off. "How do you know he was looking at me? Maybe he was watching the gulls."

"Who watches sea gulls when the beach is full of babes like you?"

"Babes, ugh. Do you know how much women detest being called babes?"

"It was a compliment."

She snapped the towel at him. "Nope."

"Guess I know now."

Alex turned and tilted her chin up with his forefinger. The sun was blinding bright, glinting off his wet hair. He leaned down, obscuring the light and Mara's awareness of anything but him. His lips brushed lightly across hers.

When he lifted his head, she had to squint to bring his face back into focus. He wore a pensive smile.

"What was that for?" she asked.

"I don't know. You had that disgruntled expression on your face, the one where you bite your lip and wrinkle your nose."

"I don't do that." She made a concerted effort to relax her facial muscles.

"Sure you do. You always have when you're unhappy but not quite mad. You know the babe thing *was* a compliment."

"Yeah. It's just that I had this strange feeling while you were swimming that someone was watching me. It made me touchy."

Alex draped his T-shirt around his neck and his arm around her shoulders. "Do you need to observe more or should we head back to the cabana to change for the barbeque?"

Mara checked the time on her Blackberry. "Actually, I have to get back to the ship."

"You're ditching the pig roast and the moonlit walk on the beach I have planned?" He waggled his eyebrows suggestively.

Mara's knees went a little weak, even though she knew he was teasing. He was teasing, wasn't he?

"Work," she said. "I'm supposed to get a take on why people stayed on board, whether they enjoyed the activities, you know."

"I guess I could go back with you." He looked longingly at the spits set up near the cabana.

"A pig roast and rock concert on the beach. Bridge

tournament on the ship. Which one would I go to if I had a choice?"

"A bridge tournament, for real?"

"It's one of the events planned. There's also a dinner theater that I'm supposed to make." She pulled her Blackberry from a pocket of her bag and checked the time. "Spamalot."

"Good choice. I caught it in New York with David Hyde Pierce. He's from Saratoga, you know."

The soft tropical wind brought a whiff of the suckling pig roasting over the fires, and Alex's stomach grumbled. He gazed over at the roasting pits.

"Go ahead and stay," she said.

"You don't care?"

Now, that was a loaded question. Sure she'd rather he come with her. But because he wanted to. "No, I'm good. It's my work. No need for you to give up your fun for it."

"Okay. See you later?"

"Maybe not until tomorrow."

Was that disappointment in his eyes or hopefulness on her part?

"We're still on for the seminar in the morning?" she asked.

"Sure thing. I want to see what Jack's made of—professionally, that is." His voice was aggressive despite the qualifier.

What was up with him and Jack? It wasn't like she had any interest in Jack or Jack in her. Or, for all she knew, that Alex had any interest in her—beyond a pleasant propensity for kissing. That could just be his way. He used to be a player and they *were* on a romantic cruise. His animosity toward Jack could be totally professional competition. She shook her head. She was analyzing way too much.

"What?" Alex asked. "You don't want me to test Jack? What does a corporate attorney know about estate planning? I'd like to see the people at the seminar get useful information out of it. If he doesn't give it. I can."

Yep, some kind of professional competition. "But aren't you a corporate attorney too?" she asked.

"Not when I can help it. I try to leave that to T.J. and Jace."

She laughed. "Whatever. I'll catch you in the morning." On impulse, she rose up on her toes and gave him a quick peck on the lips before turning and heading toward the dock. No reason Alex should have the exclusive on kissing.

Alex tapped his forefinger to his lips as he watched her walk away. Tiffani was right about one thing, the little red bikini was perfect on Mara. And it amply showed that, his baby sister's best friend or not, she was no kid anymore. He whistled as he went to meet the others at the cabana. If he knew Mara, and he thought he did, then her chaste little peck meant she *was* still interested in him. The attraction wasn't only his libido.

But was that what it was on Mara's part? A five-day cruise-ship flirtation? Candy said she'd ditched her grad school boyfriend because she didn't believe long-distance relationships could last. And no question, northern New York was long-distance from Asheville, North Carolina. He could do a flirtation. After his broken engagement, he'd sworn that's all he would do. But now, he didn't want whatever was starting between him and Mara to end when they debarked tomorrow evening.

Chapter Eight

"**R**eady?" Mara tapped Alex on the shoulder.

"Hey," he said, placing the breakfast sausage he'd been about to eat back on his plate. "How did I miss you?"

"You didn't. I overslept."

He pulled out the chair next to him for her. "Big night of bridge?"

"Totally." She rested her hand on the back of the chair, but didn't sit. "You wouldn't believe how cutthroat bridge players are. We were in it to the bitter end."

"In it? You played?"

"Yeah," she admitted sheepishly. "My grandparents, Dad's parents, were huge bridge players. Kate and I always spent a couple of weeks with them each summer."

"I remember. Candy was always even more of a pain then without you to distract her." He grinned and checked his watch. "You'd better grab some breakfast if you want to have time to eat before the seminar."

She rocked the chair with her hand. "I'll just have a coffee. Take it with me."

"Coffee isn't breakfast. I have raspberry scones."

He did. Two of them. Alex broke one in half and slathered it in butter. The warm aroma of raspberries and cream tickled her nose. Her stomach rumbled. He didn't need two.

"Okay." She reached for it. "But I don't have coffee."

"I can take care of that." He motioned to one of the servers, who came right over and poured her coffee.

"You know, I usually have mocha," she said between bites.

"Shut up and eat." With a wide grin, he placed the other scone on her napkin and pushed the butter plate toward her. "I don't want to be late."

"And you were mocking me about bridge? On a scale of one to ten, or any scale, bridge has got to score higher than a seminar on estate planning."

Hurt clouded his face, and he gave his breakfast sausage a vicious slice.

"Hey, sorry. You really like the stuff, don't you?" She licked a dollop of raspberry sauce off the tip of her finger and picked up the other scone.

"That and other things." He stared at her lips, his expression warm and wistful.

Mara grasped her coffee in both hands and took a big gulp.

Alex put his fork down on the plate. "Ready?"

She finished her coffee. "Yeah, we want to get a good seat."

"Stop mocking me," he warned. "Where are we going?"

"You didn't check? I thought you had every detail of the seminar committed to memory."

"Only the important parts, like the content, so I can refute anything stupid Jack says."

She shook her head. "The conference room on the Promenade deck."

When they entered the room, Mara was surprised at how full it was.

"There are two seats right up front," Alex pointed out.

She glanced from the vacant seats to the podium. "Promise not to be obnoxious?"

"Me?" He pointed to his chest.

"I guess I can only expect so much." She walked to the front of the room.

While people chatted around them, Alex took the seat next to her and started leafing through the handout on the table in front of him. His lips tightened and lines furrowed his forehead.

The room quieted when Jack walked up to the podium. "Good morning," he said. "I'm Jack Strickland from GHC legal team. I'm glad you decided to join me this morning for my seminar on planning your estate." Jack clicked the remote he held in his hand and "Planning Your Estate with Jack Strickland" appeared on the screen behind him.

"How creative," Alex murmured.

Jack looked at them.

"Shush. He hasn't even started."

"Let's begin," Jack said, "with a look at the estate tax."

Alex scanned the audience. This was going to be fun. "You know that estate tax is irrelevant to most of the people in here," he whispered.

She glared at him.

"Look, right there." He pointed at the new screen that had appeared.

"So," Jack said, "if the value of all the property you own is greater than 3.5 million dollars, you will be subject to estate tax." Jack continued to discuss the intricacies of the federal gift and estate tax. "And now for some strategies to help avoid these taxes."

Several people got up and left.

"As if any of this relates to most of the people here," Alex said. "Why is he wasting people's time?"

Jack looked directly at Alex, then panned the room before he clicked to the next screen.

Mara kicked Alex's foot under the table.

"What? How many people here do you think have three mil plus?"

She answered him with a sour look and scribbled something in the margin of her handout.

Alex started doodling on his, too, half listening to

Jack droning on. It wasn't that he was saying anything wrong. He just had the wrong seminar for the audience. GHC must do demographics for their cruises. He should ask Mara. Alex leaned over. She was jotting away. He'd ask her later.

"Of course," Jack said, "taxes are only part of planning your estate."

"Yeah, the least important part."

"Would you stop already?" Mara whispered.

"He's used three-quarters of the seminar talking about stuff no one here can use."

"Down front, do you have a question?" Jack's voice had a definite edge.

"I—" Alex started.

Mara cringed.

He couldn't remember fearless Mara cringing at anything. At least, not a thing he and his brothers had ever come up with to terrorize her and his sister. Did she like the guy after all? Nah, he was old enough to be her father and a lawyer on top of that. It must be her job. She must be nervous about her job. Yeah, Jack seemed the type who might jeopardize someone's job if they did something he didn't like.

"I'll ask later when you're taking questions."

Jack's lip twisted in distain.

"Go ahead." Alex couldn't stop himself. "I think you were about to use your last few minutes telling us some of the basics we need to plan our estates, like the need to have a will." He nodded at the podium.

Jack turned sharply toward the screen and punched the button to change to the next screen. "Everyone needs a will. A will . . ."

Alex leaned back in his chair and crossed his arms. A sharp blow to the leg of his chair jarred him from his gloat.

"Ouch," Mara said pinking.

He glanced under the table at her glitter-painted toenails that matched the thong of her flip flops. Kicking the chair leg must have really hurt. He had a sudden urge to lift her foot to his lap and massage away the pain. Somehow, he thought, that probably wouldn't earn him any more points with Mara than his remarks about Jack's presentation had. Alex half-listened to the rest of Jack's spiel, jotting down questions to ask when he finished.

Jack wrapped up his talk. "Now, does anyone have questions? We have a few minutes left."

Alex started to raise his hand. Mara stopped him by placing her hand on his forearm. She looked pointedly at the words he had written on the back of his handout. "What are you doing?"

"Having some fun," he answered.

"Well, have your fun after I leave." She scooped up her handout, shoved her pen in her bag, and left.

Whoa! Not the reaction he expected. Mara used to be the first one ready for a good prank. As he rose to leave, Alex made brief eye contact with Jack. He looked about as happy as Mara had before she'd left. Alex caught up with Mara just outside the meeting room.

"Hey, sorry." He touched her elbow. "I wasn't going to be *too* obnoxious."

Mara's lips curved up in a skeptical smile.

"Honest." He raised his hands. "But you do know he didn't do a good job of covering his topic. You're going to say that in your report."

"I don't know."

"Take my word for it."

Her smile faded.

"What's wrong?" He grabbed her hand and led her to a pair of deck chairs. "Come on, sit down, tell me."

She sank into one of the chairs. "You, Jack."

Now that was real clear. He sat in the chair next to her.

"He wasn't talking to his audience, you know." Alex couldn't keep the defensive tone out of his voice.

She nodded slightly. "I'll have to write that up, but—"

"But what? It's your job."

"Exactly."

He wrinkled his forehead. He was lost. She was going to do her job. And if it reflected badly on Jack, so much the better in his opinion.

She chipped at the nail on her little finger. "I don't know who Jack is." She hesitated. "At GHC. I had a weird feeling about him yesterday."

He leaned forward, elbows on knees. "I've thought he's weird right along."

She slapped one elbow out from under him. "Be nice."

"I am. Always." He sat back and crossed his ankle across his knee.

"No, you're incorrigible."

"You care what Jack thinks?" He ground his back molars at the thought that she might.

"I care that he could put in a bad word for me at work."

Yes! He didn't really think she was interested in Jack. "You like your job?"

"I like being on my own."

"That wasn't my question."

"I like the job. So far, I like it even better than the management-track assistant activity director job that I had before it."

"What's the worst you think Jack could do?"

She crossed and uncrossed her legs. "I don't know. I'm just getting settled in at work. I was kind of freaked when I had to switch to the PR group. I'm not up for another change."

"What happened?

"The woman who I replaced wasn't supposed to come back from maternity leave."

"But she did," he finished.

"Yep. My boss pulled some strings to get me transferred to the PR group."

"There you go!" He pointed his finger at her. "You have a good work record at GHC."

"I don't know." Mara was uncharacteristically subdued. "Like I said, I'm getting weird vibes from Jack. I don't have much to fall back on if I have to look for a new job. And I'm not going back home to Harmony Hills to have my mother personally arrange a marriage for me."

"I know some very eligible attorneys."

One corner of her mouth turned up in a half-smile. "They wouldn't be named T.J. and Jason by any chance, would they?"

Alex unconsciously clenched and unclenched his fists at her mention of his brothers. What about him? Hadn't *The Saratogian's* photo of him and other members of the bar association at that benefit gala identified him as one of Saratoga's most eligible bachelor's out on the town? He shook off the inanity of his ego.

"I wouldn't sweat it," he encouraged her. "I doubt Jack has that kind of power. He's probably some middle management drone who's all puffed up because he got to do this cruise gig."

"Easy for you to say. You have employment for life."

"Yeah, whether I want it or not."

She tilted her head in question.

"Price, Price & Price." He emphasized the last word. I'm number three. Always the little brother. The practice was all set up before I even started law school."

"You don't like working with your brothers?"

"No, I do. But I'd like some say in what kind of law I practice." The bitterness in his voice surprised him.

"Poor little Alex." She patted his hand.

He would have felt belittled if he didn't like the softness of her skin touching his so much.

"Candy always thought you'd end up in D.C. after law school."

"Candy always hoped I'd stay in D.C.," he corrected, "because she wanted to go to Georgetown and thought it would be an easier sell to Dad if I lived there."

"Then your dad had his heart attack."

"Yeah." His chest constricted. Even though it had been more than five years, the horror of his always-healthy, always-there-for-them father suddenly being at death's door still knocked the breath out of him. Their mother had died when he was in middle school. Loosing his father too, at a young age would have been crushing.

"And you came back to Harmony Hills and Candy decided to stay close and go to school in Albany."

"I was ready to come back after my judge internship anyway. I guess that despite my polish I'm more of a small-town kind of guy. Saratoga Springs suits me fine."

"Polish?"

"My time in D.C. adds a little class to the practice, if I do say so myself."

"And T.J. and Jace would say . . . ?" She laughed.

"A lot. They always have a lot to say. About what I should be doing. How I should be doing it. I really thought I had them with my engagement."

"Had them, how?"

"I was engaged before either of them. Was going to be married first. I thought it was about time I did something first."

"Ah, you were in love with the idea of marriage, not the woman."

Mara's observation should have raised his hackles, but it was too true. "Pitiful, huh? You know, Laura accepted my proposal because I represented security. The security that's sucking all the fun out of me. But it wasn't enough to actually marry me."

"Yes." She rubbed his back. "That's what I keep telling my mother. By email. It's so much less stressful than phoning. And anyway, Laura's a fool.

"Hey, what does that say about me? She wasn't that bad. You don't really know her. We didn't fit. That's all."

"Nah, I met her. Laura is a witch. No reflection on you," Mara added.

"Okay, she is." So why did he feel like a failure— again. Mara was right, sort of. She was right about him and Laura not being a match, definitely. Time to end this subject. "What's up for this afternoon?" he asked.

"I'm headed to the spa. Wanna come?"

"Girls, facials, and a masseur named Sven. No thanks. I think I'll take Tiff up on her rock climbing.

"So, you're done avoiding her? My job is finished?"

"Surfer dude is coming too."

"You know, we're going to slip up and call him that to his face."

"Probably." He shrugged.

"Alex," she admonished. "He has a name."

Alex grinned. "Can you tell me what it is?"

She crinkled her forehead and chewed on her lower lip.

He leaned closer drawn by a sudden urge to kiss her out of her misery.

"I don't know." She laughed, breaking the thread pulling him to her. "I really don't know."

He sat back. "See."

"I feel badly. We've been hanging with them for most of the past couple days."

"But it's not like we'll be for much longer." His chest constricted and he knew it wasn't because he wouldn't be seeing Tiffani and her surfer dude after they docked tomorrow. It was Mara.

"True." She rubbed her lower lip with her thumbnail.

Was she thinking about not seeing him much after tomorrow too? Was it time to make his move? It would help if he knew what his move was.

"Much as I'll miss Tiffani and the rest of the dinner crowd, what do you say we have a private dinner for our last night?"

"I can't." She dropped her hand to her lap.

Couldn't or didn't want to? He'd thought they had something going. What was wrong with him? He hadn't been this on edge about a woman since . . . since never. And about Mara. Mara who he'd known his whole life? This was bad.

"I have to go to the formal tonight. Work." She lifted her hands, palms up, signaling she had no choice. "It includes dinner."

Tension drained out of him. She wasn't turning him down. She had to work. Yep, he had it bad.

"I was going to ask you to come with me."

If he had any smarts at all, he'd say no. He lived in

New York. She lived in North Carolina. And she'd broken up with her grad school boyfriend because she didn't think a long distance relationship could work.

"I didn't bring any good clothes with me. I hadn't planned on socializing."

"No problem. I'm renting my formal gown from GHC. They have a whole selection available onboard."

"I don't know." He paused. "I'm not sure they'd have a gown in my size and color."

"Very funny. Ha, ha. They have suits and tuxedos too. She splayed her fingers out in front of her as if warding off his bad joke. "Don't feel like you have to come with me."

"Sorry. Old habits die hard." He had always teased Mara as unmercifully as he had his little sister. "I'd like to go and I have to say that I look pretty darn good in a tux."

That brought a smile to her face. "And here I'd thought I'd have to wait until Candy's wedding to see you in all your formal splendor. Now I'll get an early preview."

"It's only fair. I got to see you all tricked out for your sister Kate's wedding."

"The orange blossom extravaganza? Pa-lease. My dress had to have been the most hideous bridesmaid dress ever created. If I didn't know Kate better, I would have thought she'd picked it to make her look better and me look worse. But Kate's the pretty sister and I'm the smart one. I think she actually liked the style."

Even though the dress was kind of fluffy—and orange—he remembered Mara looking pretty luscious in it. He ran his gaze over her. She looked pretty luscious in the shorts and top she had on now. And where did she get the pretty sister/smart sister from? Not that Mara wasn't smart. But Kate had nothing on her in the pretty department.

"Guess it took you to do the dress justice."

"Flattery will get you everywhere. But, you'll never convince me that that dress wasn't god-awful." She uncrossed her legs. "I'd better get going to my spa appointment. If you run into Tiffani or any of the rest of the dinner gang, find out if they're going to the formal, would you?"

"Sure thing." Much as he'd enjoy an evening with just Mara, he had to admit he wouldn't want to finish the cruise without having a chance to say good-bye to the others.

She stood. "See you later."

"Yep. What time do you want me to pick you up?"

"About six thirty would be good."

"It's a date."

Mara's eyes brightened at his response, sending a shot of satisfaction through him. He watched her walk up the deck and out of sight. So much for his plan to use the cruise to rethink his life and regain his equilibrium. This whole attraction to Mara had him totally off balance. His thoughts trailed back to the feel of her hand in his as they'd walked along the beach in St. Bart's. The sweet touch of her lips on his. Not that being off balance was all bad.

Mara lounged on the bed in her cabin in utter contentment. The massage she'd gotten at the spa had been so fabulous. She couldn't give the masseur a high enough rating in her report. Her Blackberry beeped notice of an IM, interrupting her blissful aftermath. She reached over and grabbed it from the night table.

Priceless: <hey, you there?>
MaraNara: <yep.>
Priceless: <good. i thought maybe the ship had sailed off the flat edge of the world.>
MaraNara: <ha, ha>
Priceless: <well, we lost our connection the other day and I haven't heard from you since.>
MaraNara: <i've been working.>
Priceless: <right, on the beaches of St. Bart if i remember correctly.>
MaraNara: <i only spent part of the day in St. Bart. I had to go back on board and compete in a bridge tournament>
Priceless: <really rough. i'd feel sorry for you if i didn't know you like bridge. did you win?>
MaraNara: <close. they beat us out, last hand.>

Priceless: <subject change. what's up with you and my brother?>
MaraNara: <???>

Mara rubbed the back of her neck that had been so wonderfully loose moments ago. She wasn't sure she was ready to share her and Alex's burgeoning relationship—if that's what it was—even with Candy.

Priceless: <don't play cute. before we got cut off, you said you got trapped in a closet . . . >

Mara crossed her legs at the ankles in an imitation of her childhood ritual of crossing her fingers to ward off any ill effects of telling a half-truth.

MaraNara: <nothing much>
Priceless: <come on>
MaraNara: <okay. we're going to a formal dinner tonight>
Priceless: <like a date?>

Mara gave in. This was Candy.

MaraNara: <yeah>
Priceless: <oooooo>
MaraNara: <stop>
Priceless: <we could really be sisters>

MaraNara: <STOP! it's no big deal>
Priceless: <seriously?>
MaraNara: <no. it is to me>
Priceless: <and alex?>
MaraNara: <not sure, so i'm playing it cool>

Cool, right? Who was she fooling? Not herself and probably not Candy, either.

Priceless: <he'll be home in a couple of days. want me to grill him?>
MaraNara: <NO! he'll think i'm stalking him like back in high school>
Priceless: <i'll be subtle>

Mara weighed the offer. She *would* like to know what Alex was thinking. *No.* She shook her head. Way too juvenile.

MaraNara: <thanks but no thanks. i want to hear it from alex himself>

Whatever *it* was.

Priceless: <offer's good anytime>
MaraNara: <topic change. How are the wedding plans?>
Priceless: <better>
MaraNara: <good>

Priceless: <can't wait to see you. only three more weeks>
MaraNara: <me too. nervous?>
Priceless: <not much yet>

Lucky Candy. Mara rubbed her palms on her shorts. Alex had her more nervous about dinner than Candy seemed to be about her upcoming wedding.

Priceless: <better let you get ready for your big date>
MaraNara: <right>
Priceless: <knock him dead>
MaraNara: <as in bore him to death>
Priceless: <ha, ha. he may look good, but he IS a corporate lawyer>
MaraNara: <not by choice>
Priceless: <???>
MaraNara: <not important>

Sounded like he hadn't told Candy about his job situation. That was surprising. They were close. Or maybe he had and Candy had dismissed him like his brothers had. The Price brothers were very competitive. Candy had been just as competitive before she met her fiancé Mike and learned to chill some. She might not have believed Alex could want to be anything less than his brothers.

Mara chewed on the end of the Blackberry stylus. Or

had Alex been shining her on, thinking she'd fall for a kinder gentler Price. He *did* have a reputation as a player. Didn't matter. She'd fallen years ago and had simply spent the last six or seven years pretending she was over him.

Priceless: <you still there>

MaraNara: <yeah>

Priceless: <ah, off mooning about my charming :::gag::: brother like you used to>

MaraNara: <log off!>

Priceless: <nope. what are you wearing tonight?>

MaraNara: <i've got the best dress, you rent them onboard.>

Priceless: <???>

MaraNara: <i picked it out from a catalog before the cruise.>

Priceless: <and it's okay, fits and all?>

MaraNara: <perfectly. like my maid of honor dress after all the fittings. btw, it was great that you could have the dress shipped to that boutique here for the fittings.>

Priceless: <for you anything.>

MaraNara: <i'll keep that in mind.>

Priceless: <so the dress.>

MaraNara: <sea green. halter. gathered jewel bust. plunging neckline.>

Priceless: <plunging? alex should appreciate that.>

MaraNara: <relatively. the neckline.>

Mara shifted on the bed. Candy's comment about Alex stuck in her thoughts. And here she'd thought Candy might be uncomfortable about her and Alex being together.

Priceless: <fabric?>
MaraNara: <jersey. fits like a glove. godet skirt that kind of poofs out at the bottom.>
Priceless: <better than the maid of honor dress?>
MaraNara: <different. different event.>
Priceless: <truth?>
MaraNara: <truth. i would have said something.>
Priceless: <i know. i may be more nervous than i thought. i'm only doing this once.>
MaraNara: <it'll be perfect.>
Priceless: <like your dress for tonight>
MaraNara: <yep. ☺>
Priceless: <thanks. bff?>

Mara chuckled to herself at the childish best friends forever.

MaraNara: <bff>
Priceless: <i'll let you go. mike's shouting something about soccer league, said i'd watch. all those lovely muscled legs.>
MaraNara: <and you about to be an old married woman.>

Priceless: <married. very. but not dead.>
MaraNara: <LOL. i hear you.>
Priceless: <see you soon. let me know how tonight goes.>
MaraNara: <bye>
Priceless: <bye>

Mara turned off her Blackberry and walked to the closet. She took the soft green gown from the hanger and laid it out on the bed. Candy seemed fine with her and Alex getting together, which was good. It could be uncomfortable if she hadn't. Now to find out Alex's take on the subject. Tonight would be the test. She'd find out whether his interest was as a friend or something more—even if she had to ask him outright. No way was she going to make a fool of herself over Alex Price again.

Chapter Nine

Alex stood outside Mara's cabin and wiped his palms on the slacks of his rented tux. He could not actually be nervous. This was Mara. He raised his hand to knock. Maybe if he hadn't made a big deal about tonight being a date, he'd feel less like he was seventeen again going to his prom. He gave the door a sharp rap.

Mara peaked through the peep hole before opening the door. "Hi, I'm all ready. Let me grab my bag."

Alex hoped she wasn't expecting a reply. His vocal chords had frozen, along with every muscle in his body. Mara had on a clingy green dress that swished softly as she turned to pick up a small silver bag from the bedside table. She crossed the room to the door, stopped inches from him, and looked up. He lifted his hand to touch the sweet curve of her cheek.

Her eyes widened and her throat worked as if she were having trouble swallowing. "We should go now."

"Yeah, right." If he touched her, they might not get to the dinner for a while. He raised his arm higher to grasp the edge of the door, as if his intention all along had been to hold it open for her.

With a slight narrowing of her eyes, she slipped by him. A light fragrance of lavender wafted after her.

"You can close the door."

He stepped into the hall and let the door swing closed. Could he be any more of a dork?

She locked the door and dropped the key into her bag.

"Shall we?" He offered her his arm.

She slipped her hand around his elbow and rested it on his forearm. Her finger rubbed the fabric, sending a ripple up his arm.

"Nice duds," she said.

"Yeah, not bad for a rental."

She smiled up at him.

"You look great too." Now that was smooth. He was allowing that she looked as good as him. What was wrong with him? He hadn't been clumsy with a woman since he was a teenager. Come to think of it, he'd never been this tongue-tied.

"The dress is great." Sure everything was great, except his technique. He could slap himself in the head. "And I like the sparkles in your hair."

"Thanks. You don't think the glitter is too much?" She touched a silver-sprinkled strand.

"Not at all. You look like a mermaid with water drops in your hair."

She tilted her head and glanced at him out of the corner of her eye.

"A mermaid, siren. Like in mythology. The dress. It has that skirty thing." He might as well head back to his cabin right now.

She rolled her eyes. "A siren, as in lure sailors to their watery death."

"No, as in so beautiful, no one can resist them."

She laughed. "So long as you're not saying I'm cold and scaly."

Relief flowed over him. He'd thought that comeback had been corny, but better. He ran his gaze over her. "Nope, not a scale in sight."

"I should hope not." Mara looked as if she couldn't decide whether to slug him or hug him.

He went with the second. "Do you really have to go to this thing?" he asked. "Couldn't we have a quiet dinner in the private dining room instead?"

She squeezed his arm. "You have to have reservations for the dining room."

"But you have connections."

"You're the one with connections. You got into the hosted singles speed dating without a reservation."

But that was before he'd gotten to know Jack and they'd formed a mutual dislike. "I doubt my connections work anymore."

"Doesn't matter. As much as I'd like a quiet dinner

for two, I do have to go to the dinner dance tonight." She shrugged. "Work"

Hey. He could deal. She had said she'd like a quiet dinner with him. That was a start.

They walked through the doorway of the Crusoe Room into a South Sea paradise. An enticing aroma of oranges and pineapples filled the room. And something tangy, like the sea wind just before a tropical storm—or what Mara imagined the wind smelled like before a tropical storm.

She moved the godet flare of her dress and smiled, re-membering Alex's mermaid-siren compliment. She fit right in with the decor. Alex, on the other hand, fit per-fectly with the crowd. He filled out the rental tux as if it were custom-made for him and wore it as if he were born to. Two women across the room gave him an ap-praising once-over. Wide smiles signaled their approval.

Mara gripped his arm possessively. If only they knew that this was the same guy who used to gross her and Candy out with his sweaty lacrosse jersey and smelly athletic socks. She'd been wild about him then. The calm attraction she was feeling now was a whole new level.

"So what's first on the agenda? Got your notebook?"

Okay, the tony allure was better when she was just ob-serving. But before her recent swearing off of men, she'd been looking for more than eye candy. She could more than accept a couple of points off the allure for some per-sonality.

"No notebook tonight. It didn't match my mermaid costume." She swished her skirt.

"You know that was a compliment?" He checked again.

"Yeah, but I expected something smoother from you."

Uncertainty flickered in his eyes. Great. She'd hurt his feelings. But she was having trouble totally adjusting to Alex as a friend and not the unattainable icon she'd had such a crush on as a teenager.

"Want a drink?" he asked, taking a step toward the bar like he was going to bolt before she'd even had a chance to answer.

"Sure, and *we* can check out the hors d'euvres." *You can't ditch me that easily.*

"Okay, I'll hit the bar. You hit the food."

She grabbed his hand. "Wouldn't want to get lost in this crowd."

"Certainly not."

When they reached the refreshment area, he squeezed her fingers before letting go of her hand. "Want your usual?"

Her usual? Alex knew her usual? "Sure." She wondered what he'd bring her. "I'll get us a plate of appetizers to share."

"Be sure to get lots of anything that has shrimp in it. Maybe you'd better get a plate for each of us."

"We do get dinner too," she reminded him.

"Ah, but not for at least an hour. Get on it."

She pulled a face to hide the fact that she kind of liked the possessive tone of his mock order.

"Well, hello. I didn't expect to see you here."

Jack's grating comment drew her attention from the spread of delectable goodies on the table in front of her. What? She wasn't classy enough to attend a formal event? She shook off her irritation. Jack didn't know her background. She must be reacting to everyone's reported spottings of him in St. Bart's when he was supposed to be back at the ship and her weird feelings of being watched on the beach.

"I thought it might be fun to go formal for a change." Way cool. If he hadn't pegged her for a small-town nonsophisticate, he would now.

"And you do it well."

"Pardon?" she asked.

He gave her a once over that inexplicably made her skin crawl. It wasn't like she hadn't gotten the eye from several men as she and Alex had crossed the room.

"The dress is lovely on you," he said in his honey-whiskey drawl.

"Thank you. It's a GHC gown."

"You don't say. I would have thought it was custom designed for you. The fit and color are perfect. Not everyone could wear that style."

Despite Jack's seemingly sincere tone, Mara couldn't help preferring Alex's comparison to a mermaid.

"Did you come alone?" Jack asked.

"No—"

"She's with me," Alex said, the stony set of his jaw belying his perfectly neutral inflection.

"Price." Jack nodded and extended his hand.

"Strickland." Alex handed Mara her drink so he could shake his hand.

Mara looked from one man's face to the other. Not a bit of emotion showed on either. She decided it must be a lawyer thing, sizing each other up for trial. They continued to shake hands, each obviously not wanting to be the first to stop—behavior she found pretty trying. A second later, they both stopped as if on mutual cue.

"Save a dance for me?" Jack asked.

His question caught her off guard. She was still thinking about their standoff. "Ah, sure."

"I'll see you later, then." Jack moved across the room to a small group of people who waved him over like old friends. More GHC management?

She turned to Alex. "Do you mind?"

He dragged his gaze away from drilling holes in Jack's departing figure. "Mind?"

Mara refrained from shaking her head at him. "Dancing with Jack."

"Mind? Yes. I'd like to keep you all to myself. But Jack's probably only one of many men here who'd like to have you in their arms tonight. I'd rather stick with the poison I know."

"Interesting analogy." She added another hors d'euvre to each of their plates. "I'm saving all the other dances for you?" she asked rhetorically.

"Of course."

"I don't get a say?"

"Sure you do. Say all your other dances are for me." His blue eyes darkened to almost indigo.

Of course she would. She didn't know anyone here except him and Jack. And she certainly couldn't think of anyone's arms she'd rather be in than Alex's. "I'll take it under advisement," she said in her best imitation of a TV judge.

The corner of Alex's mouth started to quirk up and stopped as if his smile was halted by the thought she might be serious.

"Come on," she said. "Let's get a table before all the tables for two are taken." The room was arranged with different sized tables, seating from two to eight people. She had no intention of sharing Alex with anyone tonight. And if she was reading the new sparkle in his eyes right, he didn't either.

The dinner was fabulous, as all the food onboard had been. Mara made a mental note to report that observation in her last report. They'd also found the perfect table, tucked into a corner with a canopy of what they'd finally decided was supposed to be seaweed. As the efficient staff cleared the tables, the band took the center stage.

After a warm-up that sent her on a quick trip to the ladies' room in hopes they would be done when she returned, the band finally smoothed into a familiar slow dance.

"Shall we?" Alex asked. He rose and offered her his hand.

She accepted and they moved to the dance floor. He slipped his arm around her waist and they moved to the music in perfect synch. For the first time in her life, Mara was glad her mother had made her take ballroom dancing when she was in high school. Candy had taken the lessons with her in best-friend sympathy and Alex had teased them both mercilessly. In retaliation, Candy had made him practice with her in lieu of her telling their father what Candy had seen him and his girlfriend doing. He'd either been a very good student or had had a lot of practice since then. Probably the latter.

Alex tugged her closer, and she laid her cheek against his shoulder. His tux was soft and warm against her skin. She breathed in the spicy scent of his cologne. Being in his arms felt like being home.

"Mara," he said softly against her hair.

"Hmmmm?" she murmured into his shoulder.

"The song is over."

She lifted her head and, through a daze, saw everyone around them breaking into a fast dance. "Oh."

"Do you want to dance this one?"

She stepped away and the music assailed her senses. "Might as well. The music is too loud to talk." Which wouldn't have mattered if the band were better.

"What? I didn't hear you."

"Yes!" she shouted.

A couple of dances later, after a butchering of one of her favorite songs, Mara was ready to call it a night, at least as far as the dinner dance was concerned.

"Want to sit the next one—or five—out?" she asked, fighting a particularly loud final riff to be heard.

Alex lifted his hands in question and leaned closer.

"Want to—"

The band quieted into another slow song. Her heartbeat quickened in a way that had nothing to do with the exertion of the dance they'd just finished.

"Never mind." With a silent sigh, she slipped into his arms.

"May I?"

Alex's shoulder stiffened under her hand. She looked up to see Jack standing behind him. She half—no three-quarters—wished Alex would whirl them around and ignore Jack.

"It's up to Mara."

Jack smiled at her.

She calculated what level of rude it would be to ask him to wait for the next song, so she could have this slow one with Alex. No, her mother had pressured better manners into her than that.

She pasted a smile on her face. "Sure."

Alex stepped back. "I'll be at the table."

Jack took her hand and led her to the middle of the dance floor.

For all to see?

He guided her around the floor in a flawless fox trot. Mara had to admit that Jack was an even more skilled dancer than Alex. But she couldn't seem to get into the flow with him as she had with Alex. She accidently stepped on his foot.

"Sorry."

The groves bracketing his mouth deepened.

Jeez. She'd said she was sorry. Mara lost the beat and tripped over her own feet.

"Relax," Jack said.

Super. He probably thought she was nervous dancing with him. Nervous? Not at all. Anxious to have the dance over? You bet. Finally the music wound down.

"We're going to take a break," the band leader said. "Stick around, we'll be back in ten."

Mara wondered if the band leader and the guy who'd led the speed dating the other night had taken an old-cliche class together.

Jack dropped her hand, but kept his other one in the small of her back. She resisted the urge to squirm away. What was with her? Jack didn't seem like a bad guy, unless that really was him tailing her yesterday in St. Bart's.

"Would you like a drink?" he asked.

"No thanks. I have one at the table."

His smile hardened.

Was he trying to pick her up? Her attract-the-wrong-guy pheromones must have kicked in again. She had to turn them off. Her mind raced to come up with a retort that would set him straight. A silent voice, if you can't say something nice, don't say anything at all, stopped her. Where had that come from? Her mother.

She shook it off. "Did Tiffani tell you we're all meeting tomorrow morning and sharing a van to the airport?" she asked.

"I have a car coming."

Well, la de da.

"If you're flying United, we're on the same flight. You can share my ride."

Hadn't he listened at all? They were all sharing a van.

"Thanks. But I'll take the van. I want to see everyone before we leave."

Jack shrugged. "Suit yourself."

Had Jack been this sharp the whole cruise? Or was he testy because of Alex's behavior at the seminar and somehow holding her responsible. *Whatever.* Alex had made some good points that she'd considered in her report.

"Okay, maybe I'll catch you at breakfast."

"If not, then back at GHC," he said.

"Ah, sure." Not that she'd ever run into him at work before the cruise. "See you." Mara turned. Without looking, she knew Jack was following her progress across the room. She swished her skirt to the side and ducked behind a group of people to block his view and remove the ick factor. Could be Alex was right about Jack all along.

* * *

"Hey, think I ditched you?"

"Not a chance." Alex stood.

"Like I didn't have my offers."

Which I was ready to come squash if you'd lingered a moment longer listening to them. He clenched and unclenched his fists. "Jack."

"Is strange."

"You've just figured that out. I'm way ahead of you."

"Careful. I could go back and take him up on his offer to share his limo ride to the airport."

A muscled worked in Alex's cheek. "But you won't."

"I won't," she agreed in a voice so low, he more read her lips than heard her reply.

"What did he say?" Alex demanded.

"Nothing. Really. Forget it."

"If he said something—"

"No, it's okay. He just got on my nerves."

"Now, that I believe. Let's go so you won't run into him again."

Mara picked up her drink glass and swirled the ice around.

"You can't leave." He interpreted her hesitation. "How late do you have to stay?"

She finished off the watery mixture that had been her drink. "We can go. I have enough for my report." As soon as the words were out of her mouth, she glanced around as if to make sure no one could have heard her.

What had her so rattled? Jack? Alex took her glass

and placed it on the table. He lost no time guiding her across the room and out on to the deck before she could change her mind.

"Do you think long-distance relationships can work?" he asked once they were outside.

Her breath hitched in her throat. That was out of the blue and to the point. Maybe she wasn't the only one rattled by Jack.

"I mean, you broke up with Jesse—that was his name, right—when you moved to North Carolina."

"You kept tabs on me?" She smiled and looked at him sideways.

"Candy runs at the mouth. A lot." He hugged her to his side. "Maybe," he admitted. "We do have a history."

She burst out laughing. "Right. A history of me chasing you and you running as fast as you could."

"I'm not running now."

The gravel in his voice sent a delicious shiver up her spine. "We won't know if we don't try."

"Huh?"

"The long-distance relationship. And to set the record straight, Jesse broke up with me. Granted I pushed him pretty hard to move down with me. But I was willing to try. He said it wouldn't work."

"So, you and Jesse could still—" He let his arm drop from her waist.

"Yeah, like you and your ex could still get together." He wasn't going to back off that easily.

"Touché. You haven't lost a bit of your bite."

A stab of pain almost stopped her in her tracks. Did Alex see her as the woman she was or some version of a nostalgic childhood figure?

"Hey," he said leaning down to drop a kiss on the top of her head.

Like you would a child.

"I was teasing," he said.

She had to know. "How do you see me?"

"You're beautiful," he answered without hesitation.

Too quickly. Too pat. "What if we had no history, if you didn't expect me to eviscerate you if you said anything less." *Lame, lame, lame.* She'd been aiming for light and humorous and came off as desperate and pathetic.

Alex stopped, turned her toward him, and lifted her chin. His lips brushed hers.

She closed her eyes and leaned into the kiss. His arms encircled her waist, and she wrapped her arms around his neck. For the moment, there was nothing but the two of them.

He softened the pressure on her lips and lifted his head to break the kiss with a quick, final peck. She blinked to adjust to the deck lights and bring his face into focus.

"Does that answer your question?"

She nodded, uncertain whether her voice would come out as anything more than a squeak.

A wide grin spread across Alex's face. With purposeful exaggeration, he looked over his shoulder one way and, then the other.

"What?" she finally got out.

"No Mrs. Van Duesen look-alike to reprimand us for misbehavior." He hugged her close.

Mara luxuriated in the warmth and strength of his embrace. She almost regretted their hasty departure from the dinner dance and the loss of more slow dances.

A group of noisy teens jostled by them with a few comments that would have done the Mrs. Van Duesen look-alike proud. She felt her cheeks pink as she and Alex broke apart.

He slipped her hand in his, and they walked in companionable silence to her cabin. He waited while she fumbled in her bag for her room key and unlocked the door.

"I'll see you in the morning." He drew her into his arms for another toe-curling kiss.

"Goodnight," she whispered against his lips.

"Goodnight," he repeated. He pulled away slightly, then pulled her closer, his mouth capturing hers in one last lingering kiss.

She slipped inside, and he pulled the door closed. Leaning against the door, Mara listened to his footsteps retreating up the hall.

All right! Better than all right. Out of respect to Mara and his own dignity, Alex resisted the overwhelming urge to let loose with a war whoop as he made his way to his room.

Chapter Ten

"**K**eep in touch."

Mara watched Tiffani hug Christie and Drew good-bye in the airport lobby, surprised at how close they'd all become in such a short time. Even Drew seemed less slimy this morning. She waved to the couple as they turned to head toward their terminal.

Tiffani faced Mara and Alex. She sniffed and wiped her eyes. "Now you have my email address and cell number," she said, back to her usual organizing self.

"Yes," Mara and Alex answered in unison.

"And you guys will seriously think about a cruise reunion, won't you?" Tiffani turned her big blue eyes to Surfer Boy first.

Mara had written the guy's name down in her notebook this morning, but it had already slipped her mind.

Tiffani looked at Mara and Alex. "Maybe a honey-moon cruise."

Mara could have strangled her.

Alex just laughed. "Tiffani, you are one of a kind. Count me in on a reunion cruise."

"Me too," Mara said. Why not? They'd had a lot of fun over the past few days.

"I wish Jack had come with us too," Tiffani said.

Mara couldn't say she agreed with that. "I guess he'd already paid for the limo or car or whatever and didn't want to lose his money."

"I guess," Tiffani said. She looked up at the airport clock. "We're going to have to get going."

She gave Alex and Mara each a big bear hug that brought tears to Mara's eyes. Tiffani wasn't someone she'd normally seek out as a friend, but the cruise wouldn't have been half the fun without her.

When Tiffani released Mara, Alex caught and held her gaze. Her heart thudded so loudly surely everyone in the lobby heard it.

"Go ahead. We won't watch," Tiffani said.

Mara laughed. "Thanks, Tiff."

Alex stepped close. "Call me as soon as you get home."

She nodded, giving up the fight to stop her tears from escaping. Alex kissed the tears from her cheek before moving to her lips. He tasted sweet and salty. Alex increased the pressure of the kiss and crushed her to him. She matched his almost-desperate urgency.

"Okay!"

Tiffani's voice jarred Mara from her bliss. Maybe she should rethink that strangle idea.

"We've got to get going," Tiffani said when she had both their attentions.

Mara breathed deeply and slowly released the breath.

"She's right," Alex said, rubbing the small of her back.

Alex, Tiffani, and Surfer Boy all had connecting flights in Atlanta and needed to get to their airlines' terminals. Mara was connecting a little later in Charlotte.

"Come on." Tiffani grabbed Alex's elbow. "You'll see her again. Bye, for now," she said to Mara.

As Tiffani hustled him away, Alex turned, his pinky and index fingers pointed to his ear in mimic of a phone receiver.

Her heart soared with anticipation. In today's electronic age, they could build a relationship long distance, couldn't they? Mara grabbed the pull handle of her carry-on bag and started off in the opposite direction toward her airline terminal.

Chapter Eleven

"Good morning," Mara greeted her new boss, Tim, a big grizzly bear of a man who would look more at home roaming mountains than pacing the marble and chrome GHC public relations office.

He gathered his papers from the photocopier and tapped them into a neat pile. "Have I told you what a good job you did on the *Carolina* report?"

"Only every day since I got back, but you can continue." She dropped her bag on her desk in the cubicle next to the copier. "So, what's my next assignment?"

She caught a flicker in his eyes before he lowered his gaze and tapped the neatly piled stack again.

"The new bistro at our downtown hotel."

She released an exaggerated sigh. "I guess they can't all be cruises. But dinner out sure beats the press releases and brochure proofreading I've been doing for the three days I've been back.

Tim's normally jovial expression turned as stark and cold as a February morning in northern New York.

She bit her lip. What was that about? Didn't he want to send her out of the office? Or did he think she was being difficult? Something wasn't right.

"Not that they aren't an important part of our work," she added quickly.

"Yeah, and boring." His expression lightened. "And I have a couple more for you to proof this morning. They're on your desk."

That was more like him. Maybe his baby had kept him up last night. Lack of sleep always made Mara off.

"When you finish the brochures, I'll go over the restaurant report checklist with you. It's different than the one you used on the cruise."

"Okay." She pulled out her chair.

"Then you're free for the afternoon, since you'll be putting in your time tonight."

"Good. Maybe I can get some apartment hunting in."

"How's that going?"

She pulled a face. "Not so great. I haven't found anything available before the first of next month, and I'm supposed to have my stuff out of the storage room at the resort by this weekend."

"My old neighbor is renting out his condo. You might want to check it out. It's for sale, so I don't know how long a lease he'd give you."

"Maybe not. I don't want to be homeless again in a month or two."

"You could move right in. Live there while you look for something more permanent."

"All right. Can't hurt to look."

Tim grabbed a pen from the cup on her desk. "Hand me a piece of paper, and I'll write down the name of his realtor and the number."

She ripped a sheet off of her notepad and handed it to him.

He pulled a business card from his wallet and copied the information. "Here."

She took the sheet from him.

"It's a nice complex," he said. "Swimming pool, fitness center, tennis and basketball courts. Reasonable too, if you want to buy."

Mara folded the paper and stuck it in the front pocket of her bag. "In my dreams."

"Seriously, the guy really wants to sell. He's carrying two mortgages, the one on the condo and one on the place they moved to in Florida."

Two mortgages. With her student loans, she couldn't imagine one mortgage. In fact, she wasn't sure how she was going to swing rent.

Tim read her mind or, more likely, her expression.

"You might be surprised," he said. "It's a buyers' market. You should at least check it out."

"Okay, sure." She flipped open the folder containing

the brochure proofs and tapped down her excitement. She would love to own her own place. "I guess it couldn't hurt to ask the realtor."

"You do that." He pointed at her for emphasis, then headed back toward his office.

Mara hopped off the bus at the West Asheville stop and hurried toward the main entrance of the complex. Tim had let her leave work in plenty of time to make her appointment with the realtor but she'd stopped for a walk around a furniture store near work. She had zero furnishings.

A smartly dressed woman with to-die-for French nails pushed the door open for her. "Mara?" The woman extended her hand. "I'm Jenny Fredericks from Uptown Realty."

"Er, hi." Mara took a quick step forward into the otherwise empty lobby of the complex so the glass door wouldn't hit her as it swung closed. *A little anxious, are we?*

"The condo is on the third floor, overlooking the common area park," Jenny said, walking toward the elevator where she slid a swiper card through the card reader. "As you can see, the building has high security."

Mara nodded. *Except for people like you who indiscriminately let people in.*

The elevator door slid shut and Jenny punched three. "Are you new to Asheville?"

As if her upstate New York accent didn't answer that

question. "I've been in North Carolina about a year. I just started work here in Asheville last month."

"Then you may not know that West Asheville is *the* place to live."

Mara swallowed. She might as well leave right now. While her new salary was more than she had been earning at the resort, it wasn't in *the*-place league.

Jenny unlocked the door to the condo and let Mara go in first.

Whoa! Dude heaven. A state of the art entertainment center complete with a floor to ceiling library of DVDs—movies *and* video games—dominated the living room.

"It comes completely furnished, if you want," Jenny said. "For a little extra, the owner is willing to sell the furniture with the condo."

Mara spun around. Black leather furniture. Teak bar. A massive block coffee table that begged you to put your feet up on it. Every detail screamed testosterone.

"If I got Alex here, he might never leave," she murmured.

"Pardon?" Jenny asked.

"My b—, I have a friend who would love this room." She visualized him lounging in the recliner, preferably shirtless so she could ogle his pecs, perusing legal papers he'd brought home from work. The Boston Red Sox on the forty-two inch HDTV.

"Would you be going in on the condo together?"

Mara snapped back to reality. She wasn't even sure

she'd get Alex down for a visit. "No, no," she stuttered. "Just me." And whatever mortgage lender that might be adventuresome enough to finance the purchase.

"If you decide to buy, I have a mortgage broker I work with a lot. Remind me to give you his card when we finish the tour."

"Uh, yeah, thanks."

"The kitchen is this way." Jenny led her through a swing door next to the bar.

The reflection of the sunlight streaming through the double window onto the stainless steel and glass table top was almost enough to blind her.

"The owner had it custom designed for functionality and ease," Jenny explained. "You can add your own touches to soften the look."

"Uh, huh." Mara took in the marble countertops. She'd be too busy working an evening job to be bothered by the stark lines of the kitchen.

"Ready to see the rest?"

Poof! Her daydream of Alex barbequing on the Viking stove top grill disappeared. "Sure." But Mara wasn't sure. She was actually starting to like the place. Or was she liking how "Alex" the condo was?

"The half bath is here, off the living room." Jenny waited while Mara peered in.

Upscale, but ordinary.

"Nothing much has been done with the downstairs bedroom." The realtor opened the third door off the living room.

"You're not kidding." The small room was empty, except for some built-in shelving.

"The owner used it as his office, and took all his office furniture with him."

Mara nodded.

"I think you're really going to like the upstairs loft bedroom suite." Jenny motioned her up the Plexiglas-chrome, circular staircase first.

Mara came around the last curve and stopped short. It was a whole other world up here. Bright primary colors. Tasteful mission-style furniture.

"Well?" Jenny asked from behind her.

"I like it."

"The bedroom opens into the dressing room, with his and her walk-in closets."

The dressing room without one of the closets was as large as her room at Glenhaven.

"And the dressing room opens to the master bath, complete with a Jacuzzi."

"Very nice." Mara eyed the walk-in shower—plenty of room for two. She put a halt to the direction her imagination was taking.

"The owner's fiancée was in the process of redecorating when he was transferred to Tampa," Jenny explained.

"I see." And she did. The upstairs changes made her see the downstairs had possibilities.

Jenny walked back to the bedroom and threw open the cherry-red drapes. "I saved one of the best features for last."

Mara looked out at a large balcony framed by exquisite ironwork. Jenny unlocked the french doors and urged her out.

"This *is* great. I could put a couple of chairs out here. Maybe a small table." She stepped over to the wrought-iron railing. The condo was far enough from the outdoor pool so that noise shouldn't be a problem. A privacy screen shielded the space from the next condo's balcony. The other side looked out over the side lawn.

"The owner's fiancée had a small raised garden here." Jenny motioned to what looked like a box of dirt.

"I'm not really into gardening." The closest thing she'd done to gardening was tomato wars with the overripe fruit left in Mr. Price's garden—she and Candy against Alex and his brothers. Candy and Alex's father always had a big garden. Said it gave him peace and quiet away from the kids, since they all steered clear of the area to avoid being asked to help weed it.

"I could ask the owner to remove it," Jenny offered. "To give you more space."

Mara contemplated the garden bed. The tomatoes from the Price garden were good, better than the ones from the store. "No, maybe I'll put in a couple of tomato plants or something." What was she saying? No way she could afford all of this.

"Have you seen enough? Any questions?" Jenny asked.

"Only the big one. Cost."

The realtor's forehead creased momentarily before she pasted her too-friendly-to-be-true smile back on her face. "Come on down to the living room, and I'll go over the details."

Mara followed her downstairs. Worse than she thought. Jenny's demeanor clearly said that if Mara was concerned about the cost, she couldn't afford to buy it.

Jenny perched on the edge of the sofa and opened her briefcase on the coffee table. "All of the information is here on the fact sheet. Asking price, taxes, furnishings. It comes with any or all of the pieces here."

Mara took the paper. The price was—she swallowed—fair. "My boss, who told me about the condo, said the owner was willing to rent for a while, until it's sold."

"Yes." Jenny snapped the case shut.

Mara waited for her to say more. "The rent?" she prompted.

Jenny gave a figure that wasn't out of line with other places Mara had seen in the want ads.

"Of course, it would have to be a month-to-month lease and you'd have to agree to let me and other realtors show it."

Mara nodded as she did the math in her head. Maybe she could ride to work with Tim when she was working in the office. That would save some money. And rather than getting the late model car she'd been hoping to buy, she could get something older or put off buying a car for a while.

"You know, a mortgage on this place wouldn't cost much, if any, more than the rent." Jenny slid a business card across the table to her. "The mortgage broker I told you about. Call him."

"I don't have much of a down payment." What she did have was a small furniture/car fund that she'd been building with the money she'd saved while living at the resort.

"You're a first-time homebuyer. You may need less than you think."

Mara glanced around the room. Even the in-your-face entertainment center was growing on her.

Jenny moved the case to her lap. "What about a room-mate if you think you'd be close on the payments?"

"Hmmm. Maybe." Mara's gaze fixed on the big screen TV. Yeah, she had a perfect roommate in mind. The prob-lem was he lived 800 miles away, among other things. "I *am* interested. Can I call later today and let you know for sure."

"Okay." Jenny stood. "Call the mortgage broker," she repeated.

All right. I get the idea. The woman was only doing her job. But Mara didn't want to be pressured into a decision she might later regret. The unexpected job change was enough. Not that she regretted her new job. The cruise was great. The rest had been okay, and would be better once Tim started sending her out on some more secret shopper assignments, like tonight. She checked the digi-tal clock on the multi-disc CD player.

"I have to get going," Mara said.

"Let me lock up, and I'll go with you." On the way down, Jenny reiterated the complex's security measures and other features. "Call me later," she said, as Mara pushed the lobby door open to leave.

"It may not be until tomorrow," Mara said over her shoulder. "I'm working tonight."

"Tomorrow, then."

Mara stepped out into the early summer heat and hurried to the corner to catch the bus that was slowing to a stop there.

Mara slipped her electronic key into the slot on the door of the hotel room where GHC was putting her up temporarily while she looked for an apartment. She had to have a place by Friday and all of her stuff out of the storage room at the resort by Sunday.

She fingered the broker's card in her pocket, then pulled her Blackberry phone out of her pack and dropped into the standard hotel room desk chair. With a couple of taps of the stylus, she dialed Alex's office number.

"Price, Price, and Price," a pleasant voice answered.

"Alex Price, please. Mara Riley calling."

"I'm sorry, Ms. Riley. Mr. Price is out of the office. Do you want his voicemail?"

Mara pressed her lips together in quick thought. "No. No, I'll try him later. Thanks." She disconnected the call and tried his cell phone. His voicemail picked up. She left a quick "call me" message.

Darn. He must be at meeting or something. Maybe a house closing. She really wanted to run the condo offer by someone. No, not someone. Alex.

Because he was a financial planning specialist, of course. Not because it had been a couple of days since she'd heard his voice. She stood and paced the room and admitted the obvious. She was way excited about the prospect of buying her own place and wanted to share it with Alex.

Mara started to punch in Candy's number as a second choice. Candy's fiancé was a property manager for a nonprofit. He might have some advice about the condo. Halfway through the number, she stopped. It was Tuesday. Candy had yoga after classes on Tuesday.

Mara closed the phone window. Maybe she should just call the mortgage broker. Have more information in hand when she called Alex back later. That's what she'd do. She drew the business card from her pocket.

"Yes," she said out loud doing a pirouette in the small space between the desk and the bed. After taking some basic financial information over the phone, the mortgage broker had sounded very optimistic about Mara qualifying for a mortgage loan. And his estimate of her monthly payment was right in line with the rental payment she expected.

Coming out of the spin, she grabbed the hotel pad and pen from the desk and catapulted on to the bed. She listed the items the mortgage broker wanted her to fax him before she forgot, along with all of her monthly bills and the estimated utility figures from the condo fact sheet the realtor had given her. Then she added up the expenses. The total wasn't huge. A few more calculations and she had a good estimate of what her new take-home pay should be. Unreal! It would be a stretch, but she could be a homeowner.

She *had* to talk with Alex. What if she'd overlooked something? He'd know. All that financial planning stuff he was so into. Mara rolled over and got her phone from the bedside table. Halfway through his number, the Blackberry buzzed and a reminder message flashed. Her work assignment. She'd almost forgotten in her excitement. With a twinge of disappointment, she stopped the call. Alex would have to wait. Her bistro reservation was for six. It was 5:15 already and she hadn't even thought about what to wear.

Her persona for the evening was an out-of-town business woman. She swung her legs over the edge of the bed and went to the closet. What to wear? Not much of a choice. Most of her things were in storage at the resort. There, everyone wore a uniform. She'd had no need for the business wardrobe she'd bought when she finished grad school. The Ann Taylor suit. The one she'd worn the first day at the Asheville office before Tim had told her they dressed much more casual. And the new strappy sandals she'd bought to replace the torture shoes she'd left on the cruise ship.

She pulled clean underthings from the dresser drawer and headed for the shower.

Mara pulled open the stained glass door of the bistro. It had been so worth the cost of taking a taxi instead of the bus. Set the right frame of mind for the evening. Successful career woman, soon to be homeowner, out for the evening.

"Hello," the hostess greeted her. "Do you have a reservation?"

Polite, impeccably dressed. The bistro was off to a good start. "Yes, Riley, for—"

"Of course, Ms. Riley," the hostess gently interrupted. "Right this way. Your dinner companion is already here."

Dinner companion. Mara's heart skipped a beat. Could Alex have come down to surprise her? How would he have known to meet her here, now? But, if not Alex, who?

The hostess stepped aside. "Here you go."

Jack stood and pulled out a chair for Mara. Stark disappointment flowed through her. She barely heard the hostess's "Your server will be right with you."

"Hi," she managed in a voice that sounded almost normal. She took the seat he offered. *Work. He must be here as part of the restaurant review.* "Did Tim ask you to join me?"

"No, I asked Tim to give you the assignment."

"Oh." *Was that why Tim had gone all freaky this morning? What did Jack have to do with the public relations group?* Her stomach lurched and it had nothing to do with the hot dog she'd gotten from a street vendor for lunch.

"I thought it would give us a chance to get together outside of work."

Like they'd gotten together at work? Mara had passed him in the building lobby once since the cruise.

Jack sipped his drink. Probably Chivas Regal. That was his dinner drink of choice on the cruise.

"You seem surprised."

"Well, yeah." That sounded brilliant, and so sophisticated.

"Hi, I'm Suzi. I'll be your server tonight. Would you like something to drink?" she asked Mara. "Or are you ready to order?"

"I'll have a glass of Shiraz, please," Mara said, thankful for the interruption. She picked up her menu.

Jack nodded at his nearly empty glass. "We'll order when you bring the drinks," he said to the server.

As she read down the menu, Mara searched her brain for any clues as to why Jack had arranged the dinner.

"I have a proposition," he said.

She lowered the menu. No. She didn't need this. Didn't see it coming. Maybe she should have. On the cruise, she'd certainly enjoyed Alex seeing Jack as a rival.

Jack chuckled without smiling. "Not that kind of proposition. A business proposition."

Mara released her breath before she realized she'd been holding it. She placed the menu on the table.

"I'd like to hire you as my assistant."

"I'm flattered, but I just took the job in PR. I wouldn't feel right giving notice so soon, especially after the cruise and all."

"It shouldn't be a problem. You said that you wanted to be in hotel management, not public relations. This job would be more in line with your career track."

"The legal department? I don't see a connection."

The server returned with their drinks and took their orders.

"You'd get a good introduction to how management works from a legal perspective," he explained.

Mara sipped her wine, trying to be open but totally not seeing Jack's logic. "What would I be doing?"

"Administrative tasks. Correspondence. Filing. Proofing contracts. Updating my seminar materials."

And she'd thought press releases and brochures were boring. "I really appreciate the offer, but I think I want to give my PR job a chance first."

A muscle in Jack's jaw tightened. "You'd receive a significant pay upgrade."

Visions of the expense sheet she'd written earlier and the upstairs suite of the condo flashed in her brain. She could put the extra pay to good use. "How significant?"

"Six thousand."

She swallowed. That certainly would cinch the condo purchase. But the stony expression on Jack's face warned her that the job change wouldn't be worth even that much more money.

She took a swig of wine. "That's very generous. But, no thanks. I'm sure you understand."

"You're making a mistake."

She attempted a casual shrug. "Maybe." He could back off anytime now. His stubborn determination to sway her reminded Mara of her mother, and not in a good way.

"Blue cheese?" The server appeared at their table, salads in hand.

"Yes, thanks," Mara said, picking up her fork and giving the greens her full attention.

Jack ordered another scotch, and limited his conversation to small talk for the rest of the dinner.

"I'll drop you back at the hotel," Jack said as they finished their after-dinner coffee.

Her mocha turned bitter on her tongue. He knew how much she earned *and* where she was staying? "You don't have to. I'll take a taxi."

"Don't be silly. You can hardly afford a taxi."

She clenched her napkin on her lap. "I'll take the bus then. Walk off dinner." She signaled to the server to bring the check and took her corporate AMEX card out of her wallet.

The muscle worked overtime in Jack's jaw.

A minute-that-seemed-like-an-hour later, the server brought their checks. Mara and Jack each paid in silence.

"Good night." She stood to leave.

"Good night." His eyes narrowed as if he were thinking of something else to say.

Mara didn't wait to see what that something else

might be. She turned and walked out of the bistro, wishing the hostess a nice evening as she passed. The cool night air was, indeed, a breath of fresh air after the highly charged atmosphere she'd just left.

Chapter Twelve

Mara stretched and looked at the clock. Five fifty-five. Too early to be awake. She rolled over and closed her eyes, but sleep didn't come. Might as well get up and make coffee and be truly awake.

She switched on the coffeemaker and her cell phone. No missed calls, not that she'd expected any. She'd tried Alex again last night when she'd gotten home from dinner. The call had gone right to his voicemail. She hadn't left a message. Wasn't sure what to say. *Hey, I'm buying a condo. Or, help I need you to run interference with Jack.*

They'd talked a couple of times since she'd gotten back. But not as intimately as they had in person. A long-distance romance might be more difficult than she'd hoped.

While the coffee brewed, she turned on her laptop to check the report she'd done before bed. The IM message box popped up. Candy was online. At six in the morning? Mara rechecked the clock. Yep, six. Guilt gripped her. She could have tried Candy last night. Before the cruise she would have been IMing Candy about her weird dinner with Jack as soon as she'd hopped in the taxi and could turn her Blackberry on. When she couldn't reach Alex last night, she hadn't even thought about calling Candy.

MaraNara: <hey, what are you doing up so early?>
Priceless: <up? I haven't been to bed yet.>

Mara sighed. That was a role change. She was the one who usually pulled all-nighters.

Priceless: <u called yesterday?>
MaraNara: <yeah>
Priceless: <and?>

The condo. But Mara didn't want to get into that. Nor why she didn't want to. She and Candy had always shared everything.

MaraNara: <very weird day. Jack—that older guy from the cruise—is hitting on me, I think.>
Priceless: <you don't know?>

MaraNara: <like i said. very weird. i had a work assignment. cool bistro. showed up for dinner and Jack was there.>

Priceless: <not coincidence?>

MaraNara: <so not coincidence>

Priceless: <ick. you do attract them.>

MaraNara: <hey!!!!>

Priceless: <sorry>

MaraNara: <he offered me a job>

Priceless: <you're changing jobs again? are you trying to be me?>

Since college, Candy had had more jobs than Mara could count, although she seemed to have found her stride with law school and her work at Legal Aid.

MaraNara: <nooooo! i told him i was happy with the job i have>

Priceless: <are you?>

MaraNara: <yessss! stay on topic—jack>

Priceless: <what kind of job?>

MaraNara: <his assistant>

Priceless: <like his secretary?>

MaraNara: <exactly. and he didn't want to take no for an answer.>

Priceless: <???>

MaraNara: <he said I would make a lot more, he knew how much i make.>

Priceless: <creepy>

MaraNara: <even creepier, he knew what hotel GHC has put me up in while i apartment hunt.>

Priceless: < how's that going?>

MaraNara: <topic!>

Priceless: <and?>

MaraNara: <he insisted on driving me home.>

Priceless: <you let him?>

MaraNara: <no. i took a taxi. that gave me time to feel real weird about all the stuff he seems to know about me.>

Priceless: <i'd be weirded out too. what are you going to do?>

MaraNara: <nothing. avoid him.>

Priceless: <will that be hard?>

MaraNara: <shouldn't be. until last night, i'd only seen him once in the lobby at work.>

Priceless: <so no big deal.>

MaraNara: <maybe>

Maybe Candy was right. It was nothing. Mara tried to ignore the malaise that washed over her.

Priceless: <you okay?>

MaraNara: <yeah>

More or less.

Priceless: <subject change. what did you do to Alex on the cruise?>

MaraNara: <moi?>

Priceless: <when i talked with him, he was acting way cheerful and mysterious. not like he was after he and laura broke up and not like he was before they were engaged.>

MaraNara: <did he say something about me?>

She frowned when her question appeared on the small screen. That was pretty desperate sounding. Not that it mattered. This was Candy. Mara couldn't remember a time when she and Candy hadn't shared nearly every detail of any relationship they'd had—real or hoped for. Except now.

Priceless: <he said you guys had become good friends on the cruise. but not how good.>

Yep, friends and then some.

Priceless: <so do you two have something going or is he back to playing?>

Stab me with a knife. Seeing her worst fear in print made her hesitate to tell Candy that she had fallen hard for Alex—again. But this time it was way more than a schoolgirl crush.

MaraNara: <i don't know.>

Might as well go with the truth.

MaraNara: <we haven't talked in a couple days.>
Priceless: <not to worry. he's out of town.>
MaraNara: <another vacation?>

Her heart sunk. Alex hadn't said anything about taking more time off. He'd sounded ready to be back in the office.

Priceless: <not exactly, he's off to some conference. he'd been waffling about going.>
MaraNara: <oh>

She didn't feel appreciably better. Alex hadn't said anything to her about a conference either. Mara stared at the screen, hands on the keyboard not typing, waiting for Candy to pick up the conversation.

Priceless: <sorry about that. Mike distracted me.>
MaraNara: <☺ no problem. i should be getting ready for work.>

Had her IMs during Candy's dating dry spell—before she'd hooked up with Mike—made her feel as empty and jealous as Mara was feeling now? She swallowed. She hadn't given a thought about Candy's feelings when she'd messaged her about the new men she was meeting or cut Candy short because of a date. A healthy dose of guilt wiped out the jealousy but didn't fill the emptiness.

"Good morning," Mara called out to the empty room as she dropped her bag in her desk drawer. Tim must be back in the copy room.

"Did you get the bistro report entered into the computer?"

She closed the drawer and looked up at Tim, who had appeared in the opening to her cubicle. No hello, good morning. Someone must have gotten up on the wrong side of the bed.

"I plan to do it first thing." She punched the ON button of her PC to demonstrate. "So, the baby didn't sleep last night?" she asked.

Tim ignored her question. "Let me know when the report is done." He turned abruptly and went to his desk.

What had she done? Mara covered a yawn with hand. She really needed another cup of coffee, but didn't know whether she should take the time to walk over to the coffeemaker to get one. Why not? What was the worst Tim could do? Ask her again if she had the report done? The strong aroma of the coffee she poured in her mug was enough to shake off her drowse. She took the mug back to her desk and finished the report in short order.

"Done." She dropped a printed copy on Tim's desk on her way back from the printer. "What's next?"

"Might as well go back to proofing our promo updates. No sense starting on anything new."

That didn't sound good. "Why not?"

"You don't have to play good employee anymore."

What was he talking about?

"I approved your transfer."

"Transfer? What transfer?" Mara's mind raced back over her short time in the PR office.

She couldn't come up with any reason she'd "earned" a transfer out. Anger coursed through her. She glared at Tim. He glared back.

What did it matter if he was getting rid of her anyway? Maybe this was an answer to her qualms about a long-distance relationship with Alex. Without a job at GHC, there'd be no condo. She might as well move back north.

"Your transfer to Legal." Tim's voice sounded less irritable than before.

Jack! That rat. Mara slumped into the chair next to Tim's desk. "I didn't put in any transfer to Legal."

"You didn't?" Tim rubbed his hands over his face. "Not again. I should have caught on when I got the email from Strickland asking me to set up the bistro review and to send you."

"Again what?"

He shook his head. "He said he'd been very impressed with your work on the cruise. I thought, you know, you two were friendly."

"No way. Now, back up to the 'not again.'"

The light went out of Tim's eyes. "About a year and a half ago, my assistant transferred to Legal. Or, at least I thought she had."

She straightened. "You thought she had?"

"My wife was having trouble with her pregnancy. I was distracted. Legal had a big project and was short on staff. Or at least, that's what HR said. Jack Strickland put in several requests to borrow my assistant for a day or two. I had thought everyone was pitching in. Then my assistant said something about Jack Strickland offering her a job at a significant raise. A transfer request came through from HR, and I okayed it. I thought she wanted the job."

"She didn't?"

"No." He shook his head sadly. "Turned out Jack was harassing her to take the job. That's what she'd been telling me in a roundabout way. Not that she wanted the transfer. When I didn't support her, she took the transfer and immediately put in her resignation."

"You found that out, how?"

"Her boyfriend. I joined an evening basketball league a while later. We're on the same team. When he found out who I was, he tore into me for treating her like that. I had no idea. I felt like such an idiot."

"She should have filed a complaint."

"I think she would have if I had been behind her." He grasped the desk edge until his knuckles turned white. "I won't let it happen again."

"Thanks." She stood and patted his shoulder. "I definitely don't want to work for Jack Strickland or Legal."

"Strickland is big, though. We may have a fight ahead." Tim seemed to be talking to himself as much as he was to her.

"Can't I just go to HR and tell them I don't want the transfer?"

"Send them an email so you have it in writing, and I'll rescind my approval."

"Will that take care of it?"

"It should stop the transfer."

"Good." Relief flowed through her.

"Be ready," he warned, stopping the flow. "Strickland could requisition your services anyway. All he has to do is convince HR that he has a business need greater than my department's need for your time."

"He could do that?"

Tim blew his breath out in a poof. "He could. On a temporary basis. And who knows what might be considered temporary."

"He's that big?"

"He's that big. But know that I'm behind you."

"I appreciate it." Not that it may make any difference. She hated doubting Tim, but obviously Jack outranked him and then some.

Tim's eyes brightened. "Did you see the condo?"

"Yes. It's everything you said it was, even about the affordability, and I can rent it right away. I'm going to move my stuff out of the resort storage this weekend."

"Super."

It had been super when she knew she had a secure job that didn't involve Jack Strickland.

"Let me know if you need any help. We aren't doing anything special this weekend."

"I don't have much. But sure, I'll give you a call if I do."

"Here are the proofs." He handed her a pile of color printouts. "It really is all I have for you today," he said apologetically.

That lack of other work didn't bode well for her.

"We have the meeting with the retirement plan provider after lunch," he reminded her.

"Yeah." But what good would it do her to know what her new retirement plan investment options were if she wasn't going to be working for GHC?

She carried the printouts to her desk. The urge to call Alex was almost overwhelming. But what would she say? *No need to worry about making this long-distance thing work since I'll probably be showing up on your doorstep unemployed any day now?* She pulled a red pen from the cup on her desk and started reading.

Chapter Thirteen

Mara rummaged through the leftovers in the minifridge in her hotel room. Nothing looked worth the effort of heating up in the microwave. Going downstairs to the café for breakfast didn't have any attraction either. Her cell phone chimed. She swung the fridge door shut and crossed the room to answer the call. Probably Tim checking in to see if she needed his help moving her stuff.

Her heart raced when she recognized Alex's cell phone number on the caller ID. "Hey."

"Hi."

She settled crossed-legged on the bed and breathed slowly and deeply so that her excitement at hearing from him wouldn't show in her voice. "I tried to get a hold of you." Not exactly cool and collected.

179

"So I saw."

Mara's mind raced back over the past couple of days. She hadn't called him *that* many times. "So, where were you?" Hmmm. Maybe if she lost her GHC job, she could get one with the Inquisition.

"I was at a financial planning conference."

"Don't you ever work?" she teased.

"You know, I've got to keep up my skills."

Mara's thoughts drifted back to his good-bye kiss at the airport. Some of his skills were just fine as they were.

"I was scheduled to be on vacation for three weeks and this conference came up in Knoxville."

Right. Alex was supposed to have been on his honeymoon. She was surprised he'd kept the time off. He hadn't, actually. She'd talked to him at his office earlier in the week and he must have been in Knoxville the past couple of days when she couldn't reach him. So, why hadn't he returned her cell phone messages? She shoved an errant curl off her forehead. What was she doing? Didn't matter. What *did* matter was that Knoxville was close, within a hundred miles or so. She had a van rented to move her stuff today.

"You still there?" Alex asked.

"Yeah."

"Thought I'd lost you."

Never.

"So, are you still in Knoxville?" she asked.

"Nope."

He didn't have to sound so happy about it. "On your way home then?"

"Nope."

She bounced on the bed. Could he be on his way here?

"I'm here." He answered her question before she could vocalize it.

"Get out!" This certainly put a needed upswing on her week.

"Give me your room number, and I'll come up."

"I'll do better than that. I'll come get you." She leaped off the bed, stopping for moment in front of the mirror to fluff her curls. She frowned at her reflection. Baggy T-shirt with a stain on the front. At least her jeans were a good fit, even if they were well-faded. She dashed out the door.

She'd explain that she was dressed for her move. What was she saying? Alex wouldn't care how she was dressed. He'd seen her in far worse. But that was before . . . Mara pushed it out of her mind as she raced to catch the elevator doors before they closed. Once inside, she concentrated on slowing her breathing before they hit the first floor. The idea was to look glad, not desperate, to see him.

She stepped from the elevator. There he was. Looking almost too good to be true, dressed in jeans as worn and well-fitting as hers and Red Sox T-shirt that molded very nicely to his muscled chest and arms.

He strode across the lobby. "Hey," he said.

She rose on her toes to welcome him with a quick kiss.

"Glad to see me?"

"Don't get cocky, mister. I have ulterior motives."

"I may have few of those myself," he said, setting all of her nerve endings on high alert. He pushed the elevator button and the door immediately opened. They stepped in.

She punched three for her floor. When the door closed, the dimness in the elevator triggered a flash back to the closet on the ship, right down to Alex tensing beside her. She rubbed the small of his back and he draped his arm around her shoulder.

Ding. The door opened on the third floor and Alex's expression brightened in direct relation to the increased light in the hall. She silently kicked herself. They could have taken the stairs.

"Come on. I'm around the corner in 303."

"How's the apartment hunting going?" he asked as she unlocked the door.

"That's right! I didn't tell you. I didn't want to leave it in a voicemail message."

"Slow down. You've found an apartment?"

"Better than that."

"You're moving back to New York."

"In your dreams."

Something flickered in his eyes and, then, it was gone.

"I have a super deal on a condo."

"To rent?"

She bounced on the balls of her feet. "And buy. Isn't it exciting?"

"That's a big move. I hope you're not overextending yourself."

Poor a bucket of cold water over me. He didn't sound the least bit excited for her.

"The monthly mortgage and taxes are about the same as renting an apartment."

"You do have a down payment."

What was with him? "Yes. I was saving for a car, but the condo is on a bus route, so I don't need one. At least not yet. I can wait until I get my student loans paid down."

Alex pursed his lips.

"Aren't you happy for me?"

"Sure."

Didn't sound like it.

"I don't want you to get in financial trouble like all those people who took out subprime mortgages. You could lose your house."

"Don't worry. It's a conventional mortgage. You can look at a copy of the application if you want." She waved her hand at the hotel room desk.

"I will if you want. I can look at the realty agreement too."

Now he sounded excited. "Okay. But right now I need to go pick up my van."

"You just said you were using your money for the condo."

Would he get off this financial bent? "My rental van. I have to move my stuff out of the resort storage this weekend. I told you the last time we talked, before you fell off the face of the earth. I was worried about where I was going to move it to."

He looked down at his mocs. "Oh yeah. I remember. What do you mean, fell off the face of the earth?"

"I called your office right after I saw the condo. To get your opinion."

He nodded.

"Your office didn't seem to know where you were. I tried your home and cell phones." Jeez. She sounded like she was back to chasing him. She should have stopped with *opinion.*

"I was officially still on vacation. And . . ." He avoided eye contact. "I forgot my cell charger. I bought a new one in Knoxville."

Mara bit her lip so she wouldn't laugh. That sounded like something she'd do.

"So you want me to help you move your stuff?"

As opposed to turning around and heading right back to Knoxville? Ye-es. "Sure would. If you want to give me a lift to the car rental place, I can show you around. Where I work, you know."

"Sounds good."

One-on-one time with Alex. *Yeah, that did sound*

good, even if it meant listening to him doomsday her condo decision. She really did have it bad for him.

"Sweet." Alex whistled as he took in the giant entertainment center with its floor-to-ceiling collection of movies and video games. He finished his assessment by returning to the big screen TV. "I could be very comfortable here."

"I thought you'd like it."

"All the stuff comes with the place?"

"Yeah, for a price. The guy that owns it got transferred out of town and he and his wife bought a house there. I guess he took everything he wanted."

"Or everything his wife let him."

She laughed. "You said it, not me. Do you want the grand tour?"

Alex settled himself in one of the soft leather chairs and picked up a remote.

"Or do you want to wait until *I've* brought in my things."

"What? No." He placed the remote back on the table. "I'll carry in the stuff. You can give me the tour afterwards." He looked longingly at the big screen TV. "Then, maybe, we can catch a game."

Mara had something in mind more like a walk through the park across the street from the condos, followed by a romantic dinner.

Knock, knock.

They both turned to the door.

"You expecting someone?" Alex asked.

"It's probably Tim."

Alex frowned.

"My boss," she tossed over her shoulder as she walked to the door. "He offered to help me move."

Alex's frown deepened.

Should she tell him Tim was married and put him out of his agony? Of course, in the past, marriage hadn't always stopped guys from hitting on her, even if it put an immediate end to any interest on her part.

"Tim and his wife live next door. He's the one who told me about the vacancy."

Rap, rap. The knocks were louder this time.

Mara looked through the peep hole and swung open the door.

"Hi." She greeted Tim.

He filled the entire doorway. "I see you got some help."

"Yes. Come in." She waved him in. "This is Alex Price from back home. He was down here for a conference. Alex, my boss Tim Clarke."

Alex rose from the chair, strode over and shook hands with Tim. "Can you believe this video equipment?" he asked.

"That isn't the half of it," Tim answered. "The guy that's selling this place bought all new stuff for his new house. Did Mara show you the game system?"

"No, we just got here. We picked up her things from the resort storage."

"Let me show you." Tim opened a cabinet under the television. "So, you came down to help Mara move?" he asked.

"More or less. I was at a financial planning conference in Knoxville."

Smooth. Alex hadn't even known about the condo when he called her. But Mara would expect no less of him. He'd always been glib, except if you caught him with his guard down at home.

Tim began setting up the system.

Time to step in. "Guys," she said, "my stuff. We were going to bring in my things from the van. I have to return it this afternoon."

"Yeah. You can show me after we're done, Tim." Alex raised his gaze to Mara for confirmation.

She nodded.

"Shouldn't take us any time at all. Mara doesn't have all that much.

"Hey!" It might be true, but he didn't need to say it out loud.

"I only meant, we can get it up here fast." He turned to Tim. "I think this is our cue to get to work."

"Yeah, get while the getting is good."

"Why don't I come down for the first load," Mara said. "Then, I can start putting things away while you guys finish up."

They all headed down. The first drops of a summer rainstorm hit them when they reached the van. Mara grabbed her pull-handle luggage and suit bag and hurried back inside. She went upstairs and yanked open a dresser drawer. Today was not working out the way she'd wanted. She unzipped the luggage and shoved piles of clothes into the drawers. She and Alex had been off—almost at odds—since he'd arrived. Now the rain. No romantic walk in the park. Tim would probably stay all afternoon and play video games. She zipped the luggage closed, put it in the back of the closet, and attacked the suit bag.

"Yo! Mar." Alex called. "You upstairs?"

"Yes," she said hoping her answer had lost its quiver on its way down. She heard his footsteps on the stairs.

"We never got around to that grand tour." He appeared in the doorway. "It's nice up here too."

"Nice try." She smiled at him. "You love the downstairs. I find the upstairs a welcome relief from all that testosterone."

"That bad?"

She nodded. "That bad."

He placed the box he was carrying on the floor. "This said sheets and towels, so I figured it goes up here."

"You can leave it there for now."

"Tim had to go. Good guy."

"Yeah. I like working with him, although I don't know how long I will be."

"What?"

"Long story. I'll tell you later." No need to pile more gloom on the day right now. "First, you have got to see my balcony." She grabbed his hand and pulled him across the room to the french doors. Rain pounded against the glass.

"Isn't it cool? Like having my own little yard. I might put in a couple of tomato plants. You know, like your dad does."

"Who would have thought? The way you used to complain when Candy roped you into helping her with her part of the weeding, I'd expect you to run from the sight of a tomato plant."

"Very funny."

"What's in here?" He pointed at the doorway on the other side of the balcony.

"A dressing room and master bath." She pulled him over and swung open the door. "Can you believe it?"

"Like it much?"

"So, I'm a little excited about the condo. I'm still getting used to Asheville, but—okay—I'm really excited about the condo."

"Now that I've seen it, I've gotta agree that buying it is a good move, even if you don't stay in Asheville."

Don't stay? Had Tim said something to Alex? No, he was too professional for that.

"Show me the rest of the place."

"There's not much more." She showed him the stainless steel kitchen and the empty second bedroom, and they returned to the living room. "Now that you've seen it all, do I have a good deal? I haven't signed anything yet, except for the month-to-month rental."

"At the price you said, you have a great deal. I'd take it myself if I didn't live 800 miles away."

Alex's mention of the physical distance between them made her want to cram a hundred hours of togetherness into the little time they had left before he had to leave.

"Where should we start?" He pointed at the numerous boxes scattered around the living room.

"Don't worry about that. I have lots of time on my hands after work to unpack. I don't have to do it all now."

Alex's gaze traveled to the game system.

"We could play a game," she offered. "I'm a killer at Tetris."

"Tetris, eh? A classic."

He took her hand and drew her over to the couch. "We could do that, but first tell me what's up with your job."

A man who put talk ahead of video games. Alex was even more of a find than she'd thought. She sat on the couch and Alex joined her, picking up one of the game controllers.

"It may be no big deal but . . ." She told him about her bistro review. "Then, yesterday when I came into work, Tim was all out of sorts, gave me really lame stuff to do. Finally, he said he couldn't see giving me anything else since I was transferring out to the Legal Department."

Alex's thumbs worked the controller buttons. "Jack."

"Can you believe it? After I told him in person that I didn't want a job in legal, he put in the request to HR, made it look to Tim like I'd done it."

"You and Tim seem okay now."

She nodded. "He said he'd straighten it out with HR. Jack has done this before and gotten away with it—sort of. The other woman left GHC."

"Tim didn't help her fight it?" Alex's voice showed his opinion of Tim had just dropped.

"He would have. Said he should have, but he was so wrapped up in his new baby, the problem didn't totally register. Looking back, he says the other woman should have reported Jack for harassment. I guess I should if Tim can't resolve it."

"But the job's not worth it."

He didn't have to sound so hopeful that her job was tanking. "No, I like my job. I like GHC. I think I can go somewhere here. What I can do without is the all the turmoil and uncertainty lately."

"And Jack."

"Huh?"

"You can do without Jack. I can do without Jack."

"But can GHC do without him? He's someone pretty big. I don't know how it would go if it were him against me."

"If it comes to that, you'll have to look at all of your options and decide what you want to do."

"I *know* what I want to do. I want to stop talking about my job and enjoy the time we have left before you have to go."

He held up the controller. "How about that game of Tetris."

"You're on. Where's the other controller?"

"On the bottom shelf." He pointed.

She got the controller. "Fire it up."

An hour and a half later, they finally reached a level neither of them was conquering.

"Not bad," Alex said as he turned the system off. *Not bad. She was fabulous.* He stole a glance at her perched on the edge of the couch, controller still in hand. Her dark curls framed her slightly flushed face. *Fabulous in many more ways.* She did everything heart and soul. *Too bad her job was in such chaos.*

"Not bad? I'll have you know that I was the top Tetris player for all of the Indian Quad my sophomore year at U Albany."

He took her controller, leaned over and kissed her softly. "I don't doubt it for a minute." He kissed her again. "But how are you at War Hawk? That's a real challenge." As was Mara.

"When do you have to leave?" She lowered her gaze and chipped at her fingernail.

Too soon. He dragged his gaze away from her lovely face to check his watch. "Three o'clock."

"You can't stay for dinner?"

"Not if I'm going to make my plane."

"What time *is* it?"

"Three o'clock."

"Oh." Her lips formed a perfect *O.*

He *had* to kiss her lips back into their perfect pink

bow. What choice did he have? Once he'd finished, he backed off to inspect his work.

She slid her hand around the back of his head and pulled him back.

Her kiss was tentative at first. He relaxed and let her have her way. She wrapped her arms around his neck, and he gathered her to him. He could get used to this. Way used to it.

"Ouch!"

The word vibrated on his lips.

She pulled away. "The controller. My leg." She pulled the offensive object out from under her thigh.

He rubbed the spot where the controller had been. The soft fabric of her worn jeans contrasted with the taut muscles beneath. Yes. He could get very used to being with Mara.

"How's that?"

"Nice. Very nice. Do you really have to leave already?"

His heart constricted. "Yeah, I'm afraid I do if I'm going to make my flight."

"Then kiss me again, and make it good."

"Demanding little minx, aren't you?"

"Well, it has to last two weeks, till the wedding."

"What the lady wants, the lady gets." And he proceeded to do his best.

Chapter Fourteen

Mara checked out the airport clock. She'd allowed the hour and a half the airline recommended for getting through security. It had taken twenty-five minutes tops. And now her flight had been scrapped because of some kind of mechanical problem and she'd been given a seat on a later flight. A much later flight.

She would have called Alex to kill some time, but he was in town court this evening with Jace. She turned on her Blackberry. Super! It connected to the airport WiFi right off. Maybe she and Candy could chat. If not, she'd be reduced to playing Bubble Breaker. She should have brought a book.

Oh, good. Candy was on her computer. Probably checking her email before leaving to pick Mara up at the airport.

MaraNara: <hey!>

Mara tapped her foot, waiting to see if Candy would respond.

Priceless: <hey yourself. i didn't think you could use cells on planes.>
MaraNara: <i'm not on the plane. it's delayed.>
Priceless: <you'll be late?>
MaraNara: <with any luck, no.>
Priceless: <???>
MaraNara: <i'm on the next flight out and may be able to make my Albany connection.>
Priceless: <i've got the flight number and arrival.>
MaraNara: <good. after the wait here, i'd rather not wait at that end too.>
Priceless: <graphic of smiley face sticking out tongue.>
MaraNara: <i sound that cranky?>
Priceless: <you've earned it. how's work?>
MaraNara: <jack has backed off.>
Priceless: <go, girl!>
MaraNara: <for now. two other women, one at corporate and one of the resort reps filed complaints last week.>
Priceless: <because you did?>
MaraNara: <don't know. don't think so. tim thinks it was just a matter of time until jack's actions caught up with him.>

Priceless: <that's a relief for you.>
MaraNara: <YES! i wasn't up for a job search.>

"Passengers for flight 202 to Charlotte with connections in New York, Albany, and Buffalo can begin boarding at Gate 4."

MaraNara: <gotta go. they just announced my new flight.>

Mara stood, looped her carryon over her arm so she could still read the Blackberry screen and started walking toward the boarding line.

Priceless: <call me from Charlotte, if there's any change in your arrival.>
MaraNara: <will do.>
Priceless: <if you're late, Alex may be able to come with us to pick you up.>

Now, that might be worth missing her connection—almost.

Priceless: <he has a big surprise for you.>
MaraNara: <WHAT?>

She accidently elbowed the person behind her typing in her question. "Sorry."

Priceless: <sworn to secrecy. can't tell.>
MaraNara: <brat.>
Priceless: <see you in a bit.>
MaraNara: <can't wait. it's been soooo long.>

Mara hummed to herself as she waited in line. It would be so good to spend some time with Candy, and Alex had a surprise for her. A surprise Candy knew about but wouldn't share. The hum picked up tempo. She couldn't tell which excited her more.

Mara dragged herself down the main hall toward the lobby of the Albany airport. Her footsteps echoed off the nondescript walls in unison with those of the handful of other people straggling in from her flight. The Albany airport at night was not the most happening place. She hoped Candy had gotten her voicemail message and hadn't been waiting for her for the past hour and a half. Her plane hadn't made the connection in Charlotte.

The brighter lights of the lobby made her blink, but not fast enough to ward off a pulse of dull pain from her almost-headache. Stale air and inactivity always left her groggy and feeling like her head was stuffed with cotton. She rubbed her forehead. A nap on the plane would have been nice if she hadn't been too keyed up to sleep.

Another blink brought Candy and Mike into focus—and Alex. His welcoming smile picked the cotton from her brain. He closed the space between them in a moment, took her carryon bag in one hand, and pulled her close for a quick kiss that promised more later. "About time," he said.

Alex draped his arm over her shoulder, and she relaxed into his semi-embrace.

"Time to share," Candy said when they reached her and Mike. She and Mara hugged and broke apart.

"Did you get my message?" Mara asked.

"Yep. That's how we picked him up." She tilted her head toward Alex. "Gave him the choice of sticking around and rehashing town court with Jace or driving down to Albany with us. For some reason . . ." She shared an exaggerated knowing look with Mike. "He chose to come with us. Go figure."

Alex slid his arm around her and pulled her close to his side. "A beautiful woman or my overbearing big brother. No contest."

"Thanks. I think."

Candy elbowed her. "This is one of my brothers. What do you expect?"

Alex gave Mara a crooked smile.

Everything. She smiled back at him. *Everything.*

"Hey, sleepyhead. Wake up." Alex shook her gently.

Mara squeezed her eyes closed tighter and buried her face in his shoulder. She breathed in his clean masculine scent.

"Come on." He squeezed her shoulder. "We're at Mike and Candy's."

"Hmmm." She sat up and looked around. Candy and Mike were walking toward the house.

Alex tipped her chin up and lightly bussed her lips.

She closed her eyes and leaned into the kiss, enjoying the feel of his mouth against hers.

"You're not falling back to sleep on me, are you?"

Fall asleep in the middle of his kiss? Even a purely friendly one? She'd have to be comatose.

"No, I'm awake."

He got out of the car, walked around, and opened her door before she'd even slid across the seat to it. She accepted his hand and stepped out.

"I'm usually a night person. I guess the trip, sitting around in airports all that time, got to me."

Alex stopped on the front porch and placed his hands on her waist.

"Are you coming in?" She struggled to stifle a yawn.

He put his finger to her lips as if to help. "No. You're exhausted." He lifted her chin. "I'll see you tomorrow."

"I'm visiting Mom." Where did that come from? First, she fell asleep on him in the car, followed by practically yawning in his face. Now she sounded like she didn't want to see him tomorrow.

"Not a problem. I have to go into the office."

"We have the rehearsal at three."

"I'll be there." He slid his arms around her.

"It's the motion sickness medicine."

Confusion clouded his eyes. Or was it something else? Something that had more to do with him holding her close.

"That's why I'm so scattered. I took the maximum dose before my last flight. I had this foggy headache and no Excedrin with me. I figured I might be able to kick both the headache and air sickness." She was babbling. "It worked on the air sickness at least, but by the time I got to Albany I was so tired." And she couldn't seem to stop.

"Shush." He hugged her even closer and kissed away her next words before she could form them.

She closed her eyes and savored his taste until the snap of a twig on the front lawn interrupted her tranquility. A squirrel or one of the neighborhood cats.

He lifted his head. "I've missed you."

"Me too."

They stood for a moment, eyes locked.

Alex released her. "I'll come by around quarter of three."

Come by? His kiss had compounded the brain fog.

"Tomorrow afternoon. For the rehearsal." He reminded her.

"Oh, yeah."

"You'd better go in and get some sleep."

Despite his words he held on to her hand, lightly stroking her palm with this thumb.

She started drifting, lulled by his soothing touch. A quick squeeze of his hand jolted her back.

"If you don't go in on your own, I'm going to have to carry you in."

She sucked in her lower lip. *As if that were a bad thing?*

"Okay, I'll go in."

"We have tomorrow and Saturday."

But that was all. And she had to share him with a million people.

"I missed you," he repeated. He brushed his lips across hers and stepped back. The corner of his mouth quirked up. "But I already said that, didn't I?"

"Say it as much as you'd like." She swayed a little without his support.

"Oh, no, you don't." He took her by the shoulders and turned her toward the door. "In." He patted her behind.

"All right." She opened the screen door and turned back to him. "Lo—" She stopped herself not sure if she was ready to make that declaration or if it was the motion sickness pill. "See you tomorrow."

"Bye." He took the porch steps two at a time and strode across the lawn to his car.

"So, let me see it," Candy demanded before Mara could close the screen door behind her.

"See what?"

"He didn't give you the surprise?"

"Surprise?" Mara rubbed her eyes. Talk about sounding clueless.

"I IMed you earlier," Candy prompted.

"Oh, yeah, before the brain fog settled in. You wouldn't tell me what it was."

"So he didn't ask . . . give it to you. When you didn't come right in. . . ." Candy's words faded with her excitement.

"I was asleep. Alex woke me up."

"He'll probably give it to you tomorrow."

"I'll like it?"

"Guaranteed."

There was something about Candy's smile that said that she and Candy might have a different definition of guaranteed.

"Can't you give me a hint? I can remember some of Alex's other surprises. Like that date he brought to my birthday party when I thought he was my date."

"Nothing like that. This is a good surprise. Isn't it, Mike?"

Mike knows too? "You're not going to tell me anything?"

Candy raised her hand like a stop sign. "Don't ask. I promised."

Candy looked serious about this.

"You look beat. Why don't you crash?"

Candy too? She must look really pathetic.

"But I haven't seen you in ages." Whining. She was whining now.

"We can catch up tomorrow," Candy assured her.

Yeah, sometime between my visit to Mom's and the rehearsal dinner.

"You're in your old room," Mike said. "I took your luggage up."

When Mara was in grad school, Mike's father had rented out the house to students. He and Mike had owned it, and Mike had managed the rentals for his father. Nostalgia clogged her throat, taking her back to when she and Candy were going to conquer all, right the wrongs of the world. BFFs no matter what.

She cleared her throat. "All we need is Jesse and Ben and it'll be old home week."

"They'll be here for the wedding," Mike said.

"Yes, Jesse and Emily are coming from Syracuse and bringing the baby." Candy's gaze softened on the last word.

"Baby?" Jesse had been her college boyfriend. She'd known he'd gotten married, but not about him having a baby. He was the first of their group to be a parent. And not the one she would have guessed as being first. Not by a long shot.

"I'm sure I told you," Candy said.

Mara was sure she hadn't. That was something she would have remembered.

"He is so good with her. Who would have guessed?"

Certainly not Mara. "It'll be good to see everyone. And I'll see you in the morning."

"Mike can get us StarBucks and pick up Gideon

pastries from the corner market. They carry them now."

Mara had hoped it would be just her and Candy for breakfast. "Sure. See you in the morning." She went upstairs to her room.

Lying in bed, she could hear Candy and Mike's voices, punctuated by a periodic laugh. They must be watching a movie. Funny how the two of them talking could keep her awake when the noise of six of them sharing the house had never kept her up when she was a student. She tried to drown out the distraction by thinking about Alex. His teasing smile. His strong arm around her waist. His kiss. She relaxed and snuggled in the covers. His surprise for her, whatever it might be. Mara was wide awake again. If she were home, she'd be IMing Candy. She squeezed her eyes shut and pulled the covers over her head. Who needed sleep?

Mara walked up the steps of the duplex her mother rented. She'd slept in so breakfast had been rushed, rather than the leisurely chitchat she'd envisioned. But she and Candy had caught up on the drive to Harmony Hills. Sort of. Mike came too. It *was* his car. And his wedding the two of them were decorating the fire hall for.

She steeled herself and raised her hand to knock on the door. Her mother may have been the only person in Harmony Hills who locked her door when she was home. A woman alone never could be too careful, she'd always told her and Kate, implying that they would be better off if they were never "a woman alone."

Mara rapped sharply on the curtained window of the door and heard the *click-clop* of her mother's sandals on the stairs.

Terry Riley moved the curtain slightly to peek out, swung the door open, and greeted Mara with an uncharacteristically warm hug. She didn't even seem concerned that Mara had accidently mussed her carefully coiffed hair.

When her mother released her, Mara stepped back and studied the familiar features. Her mother's resemblance to Kate was much stronger than she remembered. Her strawberry-blond hair had highlights Kate's didn't, courtesy of her hair stylist, and her face was rounder. But Mara could have been looking into the future, seeing her sister in twenty years. She glimpsed her reflection in the wall mirror. Dark hair to their light. Slight figure to their more voluptuous ones. It brought back all her old feelings of being a changeling.

"It's been a long time." Her mother's words were surprisingly free of accusation.

Mara swallowed her guilt. She couldn't really afford to visit often. But she could call home more frequently, rather than her minimal responses to her mother's emails.

She ushered Mara into the apartment.

"New furniture?" Mara asked. She scooted around the rich-brown leather ensemble that had one piece too many for the room's size.

"Yes." Her mother waved her hands expansively. "Katie gave it to me for Mother's Day."

Mara had gotten her mother a $100 gift certificate to a local spa. Still she didn't seem to be lording Kate's gift over her.

"Sit down. I've made coffee and bought pastries from the Gideon." Her mother bustled off to the kitchen.

Mara eyed the retreating figure with suspicion. Her mother didn't bustle. She glided or strutted. But she didn't bustle. Something was up.

"Here we are." She returned with a silver coffee tray and matching coffeepot. Enough pastries for five people were artfully arranged on a china plate in the same floral pattern as the two cups on either side of it. She placed the tray on the table and pointed at the plate.

"The new pastry chef isn't as good as the old one. You know, Alex Price's ex-fiancée." She paused, scanning Mara's face.

Something was definitely up.

She dropped to the couch next to Mara and threw her arms around Mara. "I'm so happy for you."

Mara resisted the urge to pull away.

"You and Alex," her mother explained. "I was talking to Ted Price at the grocery store."

"Mom!"

"I know you got together on your cruise. And Ted told me that Alex came all the way down to North Carolina to help you move."

"He was at a conference and stopped by on his way home."

"The conference was in Asheville?"

"No."

Her mother's knowing smile knocked down Mara's defenses.

"You win." She smiled back. "I am seeing Alex."

Instead of gloating as Mara expected, her mother lifted her coffee cup and took a sip, her eyes twinkling. She placed the cup back on the saucer.

"You never did appreciate my trying to guide you toward a good marriage."

Understatement of the year. Still none of Mara's old hard feelings resurfaced.

"Mom." She touched her hand. "Alex and I aren't anywhere near that serious.

"I know." Her mother squeezed Mara's fingers. "But am I wrong for wanting security for you and Kate?"

"Of course not." Her mother was being awfully reasonable about this. She could too.

"Kate is all set. The house is hers, and she'll get a decent income, too, if anything happens between her and Blake."

Was that it? Was Kate's marriage in trouble?

"Are Kate and Blake having problems?" They'd only been married barely a year.

Her mother waved off the thought. "Oh, no. They're fine. I was just making my point."

"Which is?" Mara held her breath waiting for this calm reasonable version of her mother to disappear and the overbearing one to appear.

She blinked as if confused. "Security. Kate has her own home and security. No crummy little apartments for her and the baby."

"Wait a minute. Baby? Katie is having a baby?" Mara couldn't keep the squeal out of her voice.

"Yes, but I wasn't supposed to say anything. She wants to tell you herself."

Wow! She was going to be an aunt. Cool. That would deflect some of her mother's interest in her, Alex, and her "security."

"Sure, I won't say anything to Kate."

"Now, if you and Alex get together—"

"Mom! I'm good with or without Alex." Better with, but for different reasons. "I have a good job that has potential for advancement. I have my own house."

"I know, honey. You always were the smart one. I've never worried as much about you as about Kate."

Now, that was news to Mara.

"But, you know, it's still a man's world out there."

"Mom. I'm okay."

She patted Mara's hand. "I know, but I still worry."

Her mother sounded sincere. "Does this mean no more find a nice doctor or lawyer emails?"

"Silly. You have Alex now."

Some things never changed completely. Mara breathed deeply to keep away any hint of the hysterical laughter bubbling inside her out of her voice. "And you have a whole new generation to start worrying about."

"That too." Her mother flashed her a smile. "So, tell me about your condo. I'm sure the emails didn't give it justice." She took a big bite of her pastry and settled back in the couch.

Actually, Mara had thought her emails had given her mother a pretty good description of the place. But she gave her all of the details again, hitting heavy on the features she knew would impress her.

"I want to make some changes downstairs," she said.

"Did I tell you Kate is remodeling her house?"

Okay, guess the description of the condo was done. Mara leaned back and sipped her coffee.

"She needed to set up the nursery, of course. So, since she was doing that, she decided to have the wall between the dining room and living room taken down to make a great room and have one of those gas fireplaces installed." She paused.

"Uh, huh," Mara said. Once her mother got going, a well-placed word or two was all the participation needed to keep the conversation going.

"And they're looking at adding a sunroom off the breakfast nook."

Mara bit into a pastry and nodded. Kate's renovations would probably cost more than her condo did.

"I told her she'd better get everything done as quickly as possible. She doesn't want to have the house all torn apart later on when she's really pregnant, you know.

You get so unwieldy and awkward." Her mother drew her lips into a moue. "You're never at your best and you don't need an audience to see you waddling around the house."

No, she didn't know, but the picture of Kate nine months pregnant, thirty-five pounds heavier, was intriguing. *Payback time.* Mara had been a little chunky at puberty and Kate, just a year younger and the same height, had never missed a chance to point out the difference in their weights. Kate hadn't stopped when Mara naturally thinned out. But, then, it was to complain about how she and Mara couldn't share sweaters because Mara's were too small for her.

Mara glanced sideways to make sure her mother wasn't reading her mind. Kate and her jealous squabbles had always upset their mother much more than they should have. Mara had figured it was because it ruined her mother's picture of the perfect family. She took in the web of fine lines on her mother's forehead showing faintly through her expertly applied makeup. A twinge of remorse pricked her. Maybe Mom had been truly distressed by their bickering. All the time she'd been envying Candy's close family, had her mother wanted that for their little family?

Mara turned away and studied her hands. Another picture replaced the one of Kate. A little girl with white-blond hair and features that were far more like Alex's and her own than Kate's or her husband's. Where had that come from? She shook the picture from her head. She was telling her mother she was jumping the gun about the prospect of Mara and Alex marrying and here she was picturing their child.

Her mother clapped her hands down on her linen-clad thighs. "Where has the time gone? I'm chattering away here about Kate and you probably have to go get ready for the rehearsal dinner tonight."

"I have time."

"You want to take care to look your best for Alex."

"Mom!"

Her mother smoothed a nonexistent wrinkle from her pants. "I can't help it. It's such an opportunity for you. What are you wearing?"

She should tell her jeans and a T-shirt. "A little black dress I wore to one of the events on the cruise. Alex seemed to like it."

"Good choice. You don't want him to think you're a clothes horse. I know you have the perfect shoes to go with it. You have always been good with shoes."

At least she was good with something.

"Now what about tomorrow?" her mother asked.

"I thought I'd wear my maid of honor dress."

She laughed. "I know that. The dresses sound lovely."

Mara cocked her head, trying to remember what she'd told her mother about her dress. Nothing came to mind.

"I ran into Candy at the coffee shop." She answered Mara's unasked question.

How did Candy stand it? One of the reasons Mara had been so quick to get out of Harmony Hills was to escape people who had known her forever. She'd wanted to go someplace where she'd be on her own. Somewhere she'd be Mara, not Terry Riley's oldest or the "bad" Riley sister or Candy Price's best friend. But, then, if she was running away from roots, why was she buying a house and establishing them in Ashville? Of course, the roots she was putting down now were her own roots, not offshoots of her mother's or the Price clan's.

"You'll look as nice as you did for Kate's wedding," her mother said.

An orange beach ball would look as nice as she did in the gown Kate had picked out for her wedding.

"But your hair—"

"Don't worry. Candy's having someone from Shear Creations come over to her house to do our hair and make-up."

"Oh, good." Her mother slapped her hand over her mouth. "I didn't mean it that way."

"I know. I haven't always taken as much of an interest in hair and make-up as you and Kate." But most super models didn't take as much interest as her mother and Kate.

"Yes, I suppose that's why you cut your beautiful hair all off. Easier to care for." She smoothed a strand of her own shoulder-length hair back from her cheek. "It looked so lovely up for Kate's wedding."

And had felt like it was going to come toppling down the entire time, not to mention the itching from all the product the stylist had had to use to put it up in the first place.

"Your shorter hair does kind of suit you. And I'm sure the stylist will be able to do *something* with it tomorrow."

"Thanks, I'm sure she will." Usually, she'd be angry at her mother's backhanded compliment. *Mom probably doesn't even realize how she sounds.* Probably hadn't a hundred times before either. It had just taken Mara this long to realize it. "I'd better get going. I don't want to be late for rehearsal."

"Now, I *have* kept you too long. I hope you won't have to rush to get ready."

Go ahead and say it, Mom. You want me to look nice for Alex.

Mara stood and her mother put her coffee cup down to rise and walk her to the door.

"I'm so glad we had this time to visit. Will you be able to stop by again before you go home?"

Regret tugged at Mara's heartstrings. "No, sorry. I have a flight out Sunday. Work on Monday."

"Yes." She nodded. "You career girls. Ted says Candy is like that too. It's all work. And Kate is every bit as busy with Junior League."

Ah, yes, can't leave out Kate. She should be used to it by now, but it still stung.

"Do you need a ride to the airport?"

Mom really sounded like she wanted more time with her. "Alex is taking me."

"I certainly don't want to get in the way of that. And I'll see you at the reception tomorrow." She smiled. "Who knows? Maybe you'll be back for another wedding next spring?"

"Mom." Mara gathered her mother in her arms. "I love you. You know that." She did. Despite their differences, she did.

"I love you too, honey. You knock Alex dead tonight."

"Bye, Mom. See you tomorrow." Mara clicked the door closed behind her and walked down the stairs to the outside door. A spring wedding. One more thing she and her mother were out of step on. Mara had always dreamed of having a fall wedding.

Chapter Fifteen

"I thought that dinner would never end." Alex opened the restaurant door to let Mara walk out ahead of him, giving him an enticing back view of her in the little black dress she'd worn for speed dating on the cruise. Being gentlemanly did have its benefits.

"Why's that?" she asked, her eyes gleaming.

He draped his arm over her shoulder. "Too many people."

"I see." She nodded.

He rubbed her bare shoulder. Her skin was soft and cool to his touch. "Want my jacket?"

It might be June, but in northern New York that didn't necessarily guarantee you didn't need a coat or sweater in the evening.

"Or we could catch a ride with Candy and Mike."

"No, I'm good. I'd rather walk. But I could lose these shoes." She stopped, and he offered her his arm to balance herself while she leaned down and slipped off her shoes.

The light fragrance of her perfume drifted up and tickled his nose. He slipped his other hand into his jacket pocket and fingered the small velvet box he had stashed there. Anticipation and adrenalin mixed to set his pulse racing.

"That's much better." She looped the handle of her bag through the back straps of the shoes. She let go of his arm and tilted her head. "You okay?"

"Great." *Aside from being so nervous I could lose my dinner.* He slid her fingers through hers.

"I'm glad we didn't take your car," she said. "It gives us a chance to be alone and talk."

"Right." *If my tongue weren't so tied. I can't string together more than one word.* He stroked the velvety outside of the small box for courage. "How was your visit with your mother?"

"Good." She shook her head in wonder. "Unbelievably good. She didn't hack on me at all."

That bode well for him. As far as he could tell Terry Riley was the main reason Mara put so much space between herself and Harmony Hills.

"Maybe she's mellowed."

"Or I've become more tolerant."

He squeezed her hand. "Either way, I'm glad for both of you."

"What's this? You, sentimental? Who would have thought?"

"Hey, I can be as sentimental as the next guy."

She wrinkled her forehead as if deep in thought. "I guess."

"Hey! Not only can I be sentimental. I can be down-right mushy."

A smile lit her face. "That I'd like to see."

"Okay. I've been thinking about us. You being so far away."

Her eyes widened. "You have?"

"A lot. You haven't made a written offer on the condo, have you?"

"Not yet. Why? Want to go in on it with me?" She held her breath and bit her lower lip.

The way she worked her lip almost made him rethink his surprise. Almost. *What was there not to like about it?* "No, something better."

She release her lip. "Better?"

"Yes. One of my clients is the manager at the Gideon Putnam in Saratoga Springs."

"So?"

"You could learn the business from the bottom up."

"I'm confused."

Wasn't it obvious? "He's ready to hire you."

"Hire me?"

He hadn't expected her defensive tone. "As a management trainee."

"I have a job."

"But how secure is it with Jack and his machinations?"

"I'm handling that just fine, thank you."

This wasn't going as planned. He'd done some fast talking to convince Jeff that he needed another trainee. Alex thought she'd be as excited about it as he was. Didn't she want to be with him?

"You said you had a good visit with your mother."

"And that relates to this conversion how?"

Now Mara was sounding downright testy. "You're tired. You just need some time to think about it."

She pulled her hand from his and turned to face him. "I'm not tired. Last night I was tired. I'm wide awake tonight."

"I went out of my way. I thought you'd be happy."

She looked skyward as if he were less than an idiot. "This is the surprise Candy said you had for me? Without talking to me first, you've found me a job in Saratoga and expect me to give up a job I like, my seniority at GHC, my condo, everything I've been building in North Carolina."

"You've only been there a year or so."

"Doesn't matter."

Did he have to lay it all on the line? From the increasingly darkening expression on her face, the answer was yes. "We could be together," he said quietly.

The air between them sizzled with her outrage.

"We could be together if you gave up your practice here and moved down to North Carolina too."

At least she was onboard with the being-together part. But she couldn't be serious.

"Get real. You can't expect me to up and move. I'm established here. I'd have to apply for the North Carolina Bar."

"North Carolina doesn't have reciprocity with New York? You couldn't transfer your license?"

"It does, but there'd be a waiting period while the North Carolina Bar examined my application."

"And your financial planning credentials. Are they recognized in North Carolina?"

He shifted his weight from one foot to the other. "Yeah, they're a national accreditation."

Her mouth twisted, and his gut followed suit. "It's not like it's really your law practice. That you started it. You took the easy way and joined your brothers. You don't even like what you're doing except the occasional estate and financial planning. And you could do that anywhere in the country. I do like my job."

That's what she thought? Her work was more important than his?

A car pulled up beside them. "Want a ride?" Candy asked.

"Yes!" they shouted in unison.

Candy's eyes narrowed. "Okay, hop in."

Alex opened the door, and Mara moved to the far side of the seat. He slid in close to her. Candy was eyeing them suspiciously already. No need to have her start asking questions.

"So, how are you guys holding up?" Mara asked Candy and Mike in a tone that sounded close enough to normal.

Alex's jaw relaxed. Good. Mara was going to keep their argument to herself for the time being at least. He had no control over what she might say to Candy later.

Candy turned around to see them. "At the rehearsal today, it all seemed so real. We're really going to do it."

"I don't know," Mara said. "You still have time. Remember that runaway bride book you lent me."

Her solemn expression contradicted her teasing tone. What was with her? Candy and Mike were about as perfect together as a couple could be. Like he'd thought he and Mara were. Of course, he'd been wrong before. For all intents and purposes, Laura had been a runaway bride. But Laura's last minute flight to her park ranger had made him mad, not gut-twisting unsettled like Mara had him feeling now.

"No runaway brides," Mike said. "Besides, isn't it the groom who's supposed to get cold feet?"

"What?" Alex said covering his agitation with mock horror. "You've finally discovered the true brat my little sister can be? I thought she had you snowed."

"No, I've known that for a long time."

Candy slugged Mike's shoulder.

"But I love her anyway."

She laid her head on his shoulder.

Mara swiped at her cheek.

A tear? Was she sad Candy was getting married? He didn't understand. They were best friends. Mara's mother must have done a real number on her concerning marriage. *Didn't Mara want Candy to be happy?* He sure was getting a lesson on how well he didn't know Mara, despite knowing her forever.

Another swipe and she turned her head to the side window. Should he put his arm around her? Pretend he didn't notice? She really was messing with his emotions. He never had to think about what to do with a woman. It had always come naturally.

Alex slipped his arm around her shoulders. She tensed and continued to stare out the window. Wrong choice.

Mike pulled into the driveway of the Price family home where Mara and Candy and two of Candy's bridesmaids were staying tonight.

Mara wriggled out from under his arm, opened the door, and bolted. Mike and Candy turned to him in question.

"Too much coffee." Alex grinned—at least, he hoped it was a grin and not a grimace—and went after Mara. He caught up to her in the living room.

"We have to talk."

She shook her head.

He clenched his jaw. What did she want?

"Not now," she said. "Candy will be in in a minute."

"All right." Time should help Mara come to her senses. He stepped closer. She didn't step back. *Good sign.* He leaned down, his pulse quickening in anticipation of the sweet softness of her lips.

Clap. Clap. "Enough of that." Candy interrupted. "You can have her tomorrow when I'm busy being the bride."

With any luck.

"Tonight is girls' night."

Mara blinked hard.

"Shoo," Candy said, waving him off.

"Tomorrow," he said.

Mara didn't know whether to take that as a promise or a threat. "Tomorrow," she repeated, trepidation building with each step away he took.

"All right. He's gone. Show me." Candy kicked off her shoes and dropped into the nearest chair.

"Show you what?"

"The surprise."

"Alex surprised me all right."

"What?"

"Seems he's taken it upon himself to rearrange my life. Without asking me."

A thoughtful look passed over Candy's face. "I suppose that's one way of thinking about it."

"Hello." The front door slammed shut and Mara heard the other bridesmaids, Laney and Di, in the hall.

"He's probably waiting to ask you tomorrow when he

has more time. Don't worry. You'll like it. That's all I can say."

She smiled knowingly at Mara before calling—"Come on in"—to Laney and Di.

So there was more than the job at the Gideon? Mara didn't know whether to be hopeful or scared. If she were home, she'd be IMing the information out of Candy. She didn't want to talk about it with Laney and Di. They were more Candy's friends than hers.

"Mara," Laney said as she entered the room. "We have to talk." She plunked down on the couch and patted the seat next to her.

Mara joined her.

"You're still in North Carolina, right?" Laney asked.

"Yeah."

"My fiancé was just offered a promotion in Charlotte. Is that anywhere near where you are?"

"I'm in Asheville."

"But you like it? Are the people friendly? Have you been to Charlotte? I'm looking forward to not having to put up with the Northeast winters. I hope it's not too much of a culture shock."

The words tumbled out of Laney's mouth so fast Mara was tempted to tell her she'd have to slow her speech down if she wanted to get any on-air time in Charlotte. Laney was an investigative reporter with a network affiliate in Hartford.

"I do. Yes. And I've been to Charlotte. It's a pretty cool place. You shouldn't have any trouble acclimating."

"That's what I've heard. We're going down later in the month to look around."

"I have to ask." Mara hesitated. "You don't have any problem leaving your job in Hartford? Or do you have something lined up in Charlotte?"

Laney laughed. "I'm flexible. Jake is getting a huge raise. I may try out being a lady of leisure for a while and take my time finding something new."

"Who wants a glass of wine, soda?" Candy asked.

"I'm good," Mara said. Not at all, except for not being thirsty.

"Let's see what you have," Laney said. She and Di followed Candy into the dining room, headed to the kitchen.

Their chatter dimmed. Laney didn't seem to have any problem with following Jake. But she was following him to somewhere new, not returning to Harmony Hills. No. She breathed deeply. She liked her job. Liked Asheville. Liked having some space between her and her childhood. Alex shouldn't expect her to automatically give that up because he wanted her here. Her heart constricted. *He wanted me here.* But he'd scoffed at the idea of him moving to Asheville. She was right to be mad. So, why did it hurt so bad?

Saturday dawned picture perfect. Candy couldn't have asked for a nicer day for her wedding. All brides are beautiful, but Candy was exceptionally so. Now that the reception was winding down, Mara was hiding out in the ladies' room for some respite from being the so-happy-for-the-bride maid-of-honor best friend. She couldn't figure out why she wasn't naturally, genuinely happy for Candy. Why she felt like this was the end of something rather than the beginning of a new future, like she was losing part of herself. And she couldn't blame it all on her and Alex being unsettled. They'd been polite strangers all day, not to upset Candy's moment. But there was more.

"Here you are." Candy swooshed into the room in all her frothy white splendor.

Mara pretended to be touching up her make-up.

"Ah, making pretty for Alex."

"As my mother would say, it never hurts to look your best."

Not that any amount of mascara would fix what was wrong with her and Alex. He was turning out to be exactly the husband material her mother had taught her to look for. A professional who would take care of her so she wouldn't have to take care of herself. Never mind that she liked taking care of herself. She put her make-up back in her bag.

Candy linked her arm through hers. "Time for the grand finale. Are you sure you don't want to ride along with us to the airport? You'd have all that time alone with Alex on the way back."

"I'm sure. I need a little downtime."

"I know what you mean. If I didn't have this honeymoon thing I have to do, I'd join you."

Candy laughed and that end-of-an-era melancholy washed over Mara again. They joined Mike and Alex.

"Everyone ready?" Alex asked.

"We have to do the formal good-bye," Candy said, pulling Mike away toward the bandstand.

"I'm going to catch a ride back to the Prices' with Laney and Di," Mara said.

"You're not going to the airport?"

Was that a look of relief on Alex's face? "No, I'm beat."

"Okay. Are we still on for tomorrow?"

"Yes." They needed to settle what they'd started last night and the time alone to the airport would give them the time. She wasn't up to it today, needed more time to prepare.

"I'll pick you up about eight."

"See you then." They stared silently at each other for a moment before she walked off to find Laney.

The next morning, Mara stood in front of the full length mirror in what had been Candy's bedroom and ran the brush through her hair one last time. She'd probably spent three-quarters of her childhood in this house. Had that bothered her mother? She'd never considered the possibility before. Mara had rarely invited anyone to their apartment. She'd always gotten together with friends at Candy's. Sadness filled her. Being back in Harmony Hills was messing with her head, almost as much as the state of her relationship with Alex.

She focused back on her reflection. The cerise crossover linen tank top skimmed her slim figure and flowed in a smooth line to the slanted front pockets of her dark-brown linen flared pants. Dahlia platform wedges gave her a bit of height. She gave her dark curls a final fluff. Perfect. Hit Alex with the full impact of what he was giving up with his pigheadedness. So why wasn't she feeling the satisfaction of besting him? Because she didn't want to best him.

"Mara," Alex called from downstairs.

She hadn't even heard him come in.

"Be right there," she called back, hearing him start up the stairs.

"I'll get your luggage for you." His voice echoed up the stairwell.

Of course he would. He'd take care of everything. Now she was just being a witch. She didn't want to carry all of her luggage out to the car.

"It's in the hall."

"So I see." He stood in the open doorway obviously approving of what he saw.

How many times had she watched him in that same pose, tormenting Candy, and fantasized about her and Alex being a couple, him looking at her like he was now?

Her heart stopped and she choked on the thought forming in the back of her mind. Maybe her current feelings for Alex were actually nostalgia, wanting what she didn't have back then. If she really cared, wouldn't she be more like Laney—flexible? No. She'd gone over it a hundred times last night when she'd been attempting to sleep. She couldn't lose herself for the sake of a man, even if that man was Alex.

"Hey, earth to Mara. While I'm enjoying the view, we need to get moving if you're going to catch your plane.

Enjoying the view, huh? Her primping had been at least partially successful. "I'll take my carryon if you'll get the rest."

They stowed the luggage in the trunk and settled in for the drive to Albany International Airport.

Mara let Alex direct the conversation. He kept it to the wedding and a replay of driving Candy and Mike to the airport the night before, until they hit the Northway Interstate.

"Have you thought about the job at the Gideon?" he asked.

Like continually in one form or another.

"I'd really like you closer," he said in a voice so quiet she had to strain to hear him over the whoosh of a semi passing them.

"Alex, you know I live in North Carolina and most of the reasons why. Our getting involved doesn't automatically change all that."

"But you said you and your mother had a good visit."

"One good visit with Mom doesn't mean I want to come back to the stifling atmosphere of Harmony Hills."

"Stifling?"

"Too many bad memories. I didn't have the happy childhood you had."

"We'd live in Saratoga Springs. My house is there."

"You're assuming a lot."

"What?"

"*Your* house, *your* job, *your* friends."

"You know people in Harmony Hills, probably in Saratoga."

"Everyone I hung out with in Harmony Hills has moved away."

"Albany then, Mike and Candy. Others from grad school."

He's really not getting it. She modulated her voice. "You're missing my point. I'd be giving up my job, my new condo, my friends."

"There's someone else in Ashville."

She touched his arm, and he started. "No, no one else. You're asking too much of me. What would you be giving up?"

"I see. A contest." He swerved more than necessary to avoid debris in the highway. "Whoever gives up the most is the winner."

"No." Making everything into a competition was a side of Alex she'd seen often enough growing up, when he and Candy used to tussle. A side she wasn't particularly fond of.

"I'm not playing this game, Mara. You have no idea what would be involved in my setting up a practice in Asheville."

"I can imagine it would be a lot of work."

"Not to mention the money factor. I have to live on something."

She swallowed. She'd been thinking of them as a unit. Her irritation with him edged into ire. He'd thought of them that way, too, when it had been her doing the relocating. "I have an income."

"Be real."

"That was mean. I may not be as set as you, but you're older and I've had to do it all on my own."

"Sorry." He turned in to the airport. "But what makes you think I've had it so easy?"

"Let's see. Your dad gave you lots of financial help with college and some with law school. When you finished, you didn't even have to interview for a job. You had one waiting for you. You're a freakin' partner already."

"You think it's all been easy."

"Yeah."

"Well, it hasn't."

Maybe she hadn't been fair. His father's heart attack had brought him back to Harmony Hills. He hadn't planned on staying. But he had. "You didn't have to join your brothers. You could have said no."

"Like you." He dragged his hand through his hair. "Not everyone can cut lifelong ties with no looking back."

A lesion of pain opened up inside her. "That's what you think I've done?"

"Isn't it?"

She shook her head, blinking back tears of frustration and sadness. He didn't know her at all. "No, I was making a life for myself, not for others."

"Maybe family means something to me."

His words cut the tenuous hold she had on her emotions. A tear escaped and slid down her cheek. Just because she wasn't as close to her mother and Kate as he was to his family didn't mean she didn't care.

Alex jerked the car into a parking space in the airport lot and brought it to an abrupt stop. He dropped his head to rest on the steering wheel.

Mara touched his arm. Despite her anger, she couldn't stand to see him like this.

He raised his head and looked at her. "Sorry. That was mean too. Let's stop fighting."

"We haven't resolved anything."

His jaw tensed. "You don't have to decide today."

Despair gripped her heart. He hadn't heard her at all.

"Come on, you have to go in less than an hour. I don't want to leave you like this."

She mustered every bit of strength she had. "Alex, I'm not going to change my mind."

His face blanched before coloring with anger. "If you loved me, you'd at least consider it."

If she loved him? The last time she'd heard that adolescent line, it was from a high school boyfriend hoping to get lucky.

"But, then, you've never said you do."

"And you have?"

His head jerked back as if she'd slapped him. "I texted you from Knoxville before I got on the plane."

"I . . . I didn't get it, see it." Her palm itched to reach in her bag and check her Blackberry.

"I've waited for you to say it." He voice grew thick. "I felt your love. Or thought I did."

She took his hand in hers and squeezed it. "I do love you. I have for years."

He squeezed back. "But it's not enough."

Mara closed her eyes. "I didn't say that. I just don't want to lose myself."

He gently kissed her forehead. "I don't understand."

She opened her eyes. "I know."

His chest rose and fell and her heart with it.

He gave her hand another squeeze. "We'd better get your luggage in and checked."

A chill wind blew through the highway corridor formed by the brick walls of the parking lot/garage area and the glass-fronted terminal. Mara checked her bag, and they walked silently to the small waiting area outside the security check area.

"I should be going," she said.

He nodded. "Call and let me know you got home safely."

Mara knew he was being considerate, but she didn't think she'd be up to another round today. It must have shown on her face.

"I'll let the call go to voicemail."

She smiled. "Thanks."

He slid the strap of her carryon bag from her shoulder and froze her in place with the intensity of his gaze. His pupils were a mere pinpoint of black centered in vibrant blue. He crushed his lips to hers. The drive down and everything around them faded away as she lost herself in the possessiveness of his kiss.

Alex slowly ended the kiss. Each degree he lightened the pressure of his lips on hers added a brick to the wall building between them. A wall she didn't know if they could breach.

He trailed light kisses up her cheek to her ear. "I'll call you tomorrow."

As much as Mara knew Alex's words were a promise, a part of her couldn't help but hear them as a threat to pick up where they left off in the car. "All right, and I'll let you know when I get into Asheville."

"When you get home to the condo."

"When I get home to the condo."

He pressed his lips to hers for a final lingering kiss. "Tomorrow."

"Talk to you then." She picked up her carryon, pulled the strap up on her shoulder, and walked to the end of one of the security checkpoints, feeling she should have said more, but she'd said all she could.

By the time he got home to Saratoga Springs, Alex was sure Mara's flight would be in the air and her cell phone turned off. He pushed his speed dial number one.

"Hi, this is Mara. Leave a message and I'll get back to you when I can."

"It's me. Miss you already. I love you." He turned his phone off and thought about the box up on his dresser. Mara's visit hadn't turned out anything like he'd planned.

But she'd come around. He knew she would. She just needed time.

Mara dropped into the soft leather chair in the condo living room, flipped her cell phone open, and pushed her speed dial number one. After the cruise, she'd made Alex number one and switched Candy to number two. *Don't answer, don't answer,* she repeated in an unspoken litany.

"Alex Price. I'm not available right now. Leave a message or try my office number, 555-641-1688."

"Hi, it's Mara." As though he couldn't recognize her voice, wasn't expecting her message. "I'm home, safe and sound. The flight was uneventful." *Uneventful?* Not a word she normally used. "Talk to you tomorrow."

She looked at her Blackberry phone screen and saw she had a voicemail message. It was from Alex. He must have called while she was in-flight. Maybe he'd thought things over and was ready to reconsider. Hey! Everyone she knew seemed to be into thinking positive, visualizing what they wanted. She called her voicemail.

"It's me. Miss you already. I love you." His rich baritone caressed her ear, and she melted into the chair.

She pushed call back and waited impatiently for his voicemail greeting to end. "I love you too."

And she truly did, but was that enough?

Chapter Sixteen

Mara stepped off the bus in front of her building. After her restless night last night, it had been good to be back at work today, even if she had to triple her usual caffeine intake to stay alert. She entered the lobby, went to her mailbox, unlocked it, and pulled out a fistful of envelopes. Probably all credit card offers and ads. She'd been too disheartened last night to retrieve her mail from the days she was up north.

Furniture store ad, postcard reminder to schedule her dental cleaning appointment, catalogs from places she'd never ordered anything from. She rifled through the stack on the elevator. A home equity offer. She didn't even own a home. Yet. Her heart pounded. The next envelope bore the red and white logo of the bank where she'd applied for her mortgage. She rushed out into the hall as soon as the elevator doors opened and proceeded to drop her keys in her haste to open the condo door. Once inside, she tossed the rest of the mail on the closest table and tore open the envelope from the bank.

We are pleased to inform you . . .

"Yes!" she shouted. She'd been approved for the mortgage. Wait until she told Alex. The super game system. She spun around. Everything. It was all going to be hers. A flashback to last night at the airport knocked her excitement down several decibels.

No! If pessimistic people could believe that bad things happened in threes, she was going to go with good things happening in threes. The mortgage approval was one. The news she received at work today about Jack's resignation was two.

A loud ring blared from her bag. She grabbed her Blackberry. Three, Alex calling to tell her he was willing to consider a move down to Asheville. That's all she needed for now, him reconsidering the idea. That and him forgetting about her taking the job at the Gideon. She wasn't totally against leaving Asheville and GHC. But it would have to be the right job, her decision.

She pushed the answer button. "Hello."

"Hey, I got your message."

The sound of his voice filled her with longing.

"And I got yours. How was your day?"

"Nothing special. Yours?"

"Great. Jack's gone. He resigned rather than answer the complaints against him."

"They let him do that. Interesting."

Interesting? That's all he had to say? Not great. Or what a relief for you? Or, even, a simple, I'm glad?

"And my mortgage was approved." She waited for Alex's reaction until the silence stretched out so long she thought they'd lost their phone connection.

"You still there?" she asked.

"Yeah. You're not going through with the mortgage, are you?"

So much for good things happening in threes.

"I am."

"But what about moving up here?"

"My job is here. I thought you understood after we talked yesterday." Hoped he'd finally understood.

"You have the offer from the Gideon."

"No, you have the offer for me from the Gideon."

"Same thing."

He hadn't gotten it. Wasn't getting it. Her throat constricted so she could hardly breathe, let alone talk. She swallowed hard.

"I'm not dead set against moving back to New York. It just has to be on my terms, for me."

"I don't see why you can't take the job at the Gideon and look around for something else."

"I could, but that's not the point."

"Then what is the point?" He enunciated each word clearly and separately.

She gripped the phone tighter. Now he was being purposely obtuse?

"Do you always have to do everything the hard way?"

Her patience broke. "Do you always take the easy way?"

"You really think so."

Although his voice was harsh, it had a twinge of hurt to it. A twinge that calmed her angry frustration, leaving her tired and empty.

"No, I'm looking for some middle ground."

"Meaning your way or no way."

Mara drew on the conflict resolution training GHC had sent her to before she'd worked on the front desk at the resort. "We're not getting anywhere."

"That's for sure."

She counted to three, thinking three hundred might be needed to stop herself from telling him what a jerk he was being. "Why don't we think things over and talk tomorrow."

"You're blowing me off. Either you want to be with me or you don't."

Why did guys have to be so black and white? All of her training abandoned her. "I'm not giving up my job and my condo for your convenience."

"Your choice. I won't beg."

"Alex." Her chest tightened and tears filled her eyes.

"At least Laura dumped me for another guy. You're dumping me for a job."

Mara resisted an urge to throw the phone at the wall. "I'll call you tomorrow." She met out the words. "We've got to work this out."

"Do we? From here, it sounds like you already have—without me."

She wasn't going to beg either. "I'm going to go."

"Fine." He clicked off.

She stared at the Blackberry, all the joy from learning of Jack's departure and the mortgage approval obliterated. He'd call back once he'd come to his senses, wouldn't he?

Mara cleared her desk and walked her finished report over to Tim's desk. He'd already left, but she'd wanted to stay and write up her comments on the new coffee shop at the resort. It had been fun to see some of her old coworkers. Her cover had been that she'd won a day at the resort as part of a productivity reward drawing at corporate.

She dropped the report in Tim's in-box and looked up at the globe clock he had on his desk. Five twenty. If possible, Friday had come too soon this week. She'd gotten Alex's voicemail when she'd called him back on Tuesday and decided not to leave a message. Being busy at work helped her ignore the fact that Alex must have seen her number on his caller ID but hadn't called her back.

Now two long days of nothing to distract her loomed ahead. Tim's in-laws were coming to visit them this weekend and she didn't know any of her other neighbors well yet. Her friends at the resort had invited her to join them Friday or Saturday night. But without the company car she'd had yesterday, getting there was a problem.

Mara returned to her desk. Nothing to do here either. She pulled her bag from the drawer and headed toward the door, waving to one of the graphic artists on her way out. Nice guy, kind of cute. He'd asked her out last week. She'd told him she was involved with someone. She hugged herself to ward off the emptiness.

The bus pulled up just as she reached the bus stop. She climbed on and found a seat by herself. Her phone chimed.

Priceless: <hey, we're in country. short layover in Boston.>

MaraNara: <how was Ireland?>

Priceless: <great! everything i expected. so did you tell him yes? i'm dying to know.>

MaraNara: <tell who yes to what?>

Priceless: <alex. he did propose on sunday didn't he?>

MaraNara: <as in marriage?>

That's what Candy had meant after the rehearsal dinner when she'd said, "let's see it, show me." The malaise she'd fought all week took root, making her sick to her stomach. Before they'd argued, Alex had intended to ask her to marry him. Not that him proposing would have made a difference. She didn't plan on losing herself in marriage either. And he'd sure dropped the idea fast enough when she hadn't jumped at his other plans for her. Bleakness replaced the emptiness she'd felt earlier. Alex had said he'd been more in love with the idea of marriage and besting his brothers than he had been with Laura. Seemed like history was repeating itself.

Priceless: <he didn't. he'd planned to. really. he was so excited about the ring.>

About the ring, maybe the idea of being married, but not about her, the real her.

Priceless: <you there?>
MaraNara: <i haven't talked with him since Tuesday. he won't call me back.>
Priceless: <what did he do?>
MaraNara: <nothing. i'm not the person he thought i was. i can't be someone i'm not.>
Priceless: <he loves you. i know he does.>

Or you want to believe he does. Trouble was Mara wanted to believe that, too, with every fiber of her being.

Priceless: <jerk! ill set him straight when he picks us up.>
MaraNara: <don't!>

She'd told Alex she wouldn't beg. She didn't need Candy begging on her behalf.

Priceless: <gotta go. they're calling our flight. i'll take care of it. bye.>

Great! Mara stared at the blurred Blackberry screen. Alex would know Candy had talked with her, probably think Mara asked her to talk with him. It was worse than the disastrous dinner party she'd thrown for Alex's high school graduation. Then she'd only fantasized she was in love with him. Now she was in love with him. For the first time, she was glad they had 800 miles between them so she wouldn't have to experience the embarrassment and pain in person.

Alex stuffed the merger papers in his briefcase. He had nothing planned for the weekend except picking Candy and Mike up at the airport tonight. Might as well work. T.J and Jace had made a big deal about giving him this client. He couldn't see the excitement. But they'd be pleased if he had the contracts all reviewed first thing Monday morning.

So what? The thought came out of nowhere, as had many concerning his work the past few days. Was Mara right? Did he always take the easy route? Work didn't seem too easy lately. The past few days everything, not just work, had been a chore.

Blast her! She could have called back a second time to work things out. It was her move. He didn't throw around "I love you" lightly. Maybe she thought he did.

He did have a reputation. He'd cultivated it at one time. He gave his indignation free reign. What guy wouldn't? He wasn't a player now. How could she not see? She thought he didn't know her. She didn't know him any better. Wasn't that what you got engaged for? Time to get to know each other better? Of course, she'd cut him off before he'd gotten as far as proposing.

Honk!

Startled, he looked up to see the stoplight in front of him had turned green. Scary. He'd left the office and driven nearly the entire distance from Saratoga to Albany in a self-absorbed fog. He drove the short distance remaining to the airport, parked the car, and went in to meet Candy and Mike.

"Alex! What were you thinking? Wait. You weren't thinking."

At least Candy had waited until she and Mike were in his car before she lit into him.

"Honeymoon didn't agree with you?"

Mike made a strangled noise in the back seat.

"Mara is the best thing that's ever happened to you, and I'm not saying that just because we're best friends."

Alex moved to the exit lane and circled out of the airport parking lot. He couldn't argue with that. He might as well admit it. "Yeah."

"So why are you being such a jerk to her?"

"Me?" He hit the brake with more force than necessary

to turn on to the interstate toward Albany. "I did everything I could to make it easier for us to be together. I thought she'd come around."

"Come around to what?"

"I found her a job at the Gideon, so we could be together."

"Without asking her?"

Obviously a screeching offense. If he weren't driving, he'd cover his ears to muffle his sister's voice. "It seemed like a good idea. If she didn't like it, she could look for something else."

"What did she say?"

"That she liked her job at GHC, and I should think about moving there."

"Have you?"

"I'm established at Price, Price & Price. A partner."

"In other words, no. You like being under T.J.'s and Jace's thumbs too much to even consider leaving? You always have taken the smooth path."

"Mara said the same thing." But she hadn't been quite as nice. That spoke volumes.

"I thought you loved her."

"I do," he answered without hesitation. And he did. He'd always loved her a little. Their reunion on the cruise had nurtured that little into much, much more. But giving up his comfortable niche for love was scary. Not that he'd admit it to anyone. His sister in particular.

"You gave up that job offer in Washington to stay in Albany with Mike." He challenged her.

"Not only for Mike. I had other reasons for staying. Reasons that were important to me. Like I'm sure Mara has reasons she'd like to stay in Asheville. And Mike didn't demand I stay."

"You think I demanded Mara move back."

"Yes," she shot back at him before he'd even finished his thought.

He swallowed. He pretty much had.

"I know you. You're used to people—women—falling all over themselves to do what you want."

"I'm not nearly that bad."

"Ahem." Mike cleared his throat.

"Okay. I might be like that. On occasion."

Candy took advantage of his admission. "Good. Now tell me that you're crazy about your job."

"You know I'm not."

"Then why drive Mara off by refusing to consider moving down to North Carolina?"

"I didn't. I was waiting for her to call me back."

"She did."

"I know. I meant again. I thought . . . if she was serious . . . it was her move." Jeez! Was he as lame as he sounded?

"You should call her back, man." Mike said. "And—" Alex caught his gesture toward the window in the rearview mirror. "That was our street."

"I thought Homestead came first and then Winthrop." Alex went around the block and pulled the car into Mike and Candy's driveway. Once again he'd driven a whole trip without any memory of it. This could be a danger-ous habit.

"Thanks for the lift," Mike said, swinging the door open to step out.

"No problem."

Candy squeezed Alex's hand and gave him "the look." The one that said he was one step below Neanderthal. "Mara made her move. The ball is in your court now."

Right! If he only knew the rules of the game. Alex popped the trunk so Mike and Candy could get their lug-gage and waited until they were in the house before he rammed the gearshift into reverse and left.

Yeah, he'd messed up. Big time. Now, what was he going to do about it?

Mara gave the bookcase one final swipe with the duster and stepped back to admire her work. She'd cleaned the condo from top to bottom and spent the past hour unpacking the last of her books and arranging them alphabetically by author on the built-in bookcase. She collapsed on the couch and checked the clock on the DVD player. Six. The whole evening was still ahead.

She could call her mother, except she'd already called her this morning. And her sister, Kate. And Candy, but she wasn't home. She was working at Legal Aid today. So Mara had chatted with Mike for a while. That had all killed about an hour.

She leaned her head back on the couch and stared at

the ceiling. What was with her? She used to have a life. At least she thought she did. A life she was happy with. Until Alex Price sailed back into it—and out again. Sad. She was just plain sad.

Well, she wasn't going to sit here and moon over him. She'd already done that back in high school. She jumped up and went to the kitchen for another bowl of triple chocolate peanut butter cup ice cream. The empty container on the counter reminded her that she'd finished it for lunch.

Knock, knock. The sound of someone at the door interrupted her rummaging. Must be Tim in search of an escape from his in-laws. He'd said they could get a little intense. Some of her glum faded. They could play a video game or two. Maybe his wife and her parents would all want to order in pizza or something.

She went to the door, looked through the peephole, and froze. The knocking became more insistent. She lifted her hand in slow motion as if it were weighted to her side and turned the deadbolt, then the doorknob. The door swung open. Alex stood inches away from her, hair mussed, eyes bloodshot, feet planted a foot and a half apart as if to brace himself.

"You look like hell," she blurted.

"Good to see you too." A lopsided grin spread across his face.

Where was a good sink hole when you needed one? "Sorry, but . . . you look . . . I . . . come in." She grabbed his forearm and pulled him into the condo. The solid feel of muscle beneath warmth of his skin did nothing to calm her pounding heart.

"How did you get in the building?" She couldn't imagine any of her neighbors letting in anyone as disheveled as Alex. Not that he didn't look twice as yummy to her as the triple chocolate peanut butter ice cream she'd craved a minute ago.

"Tim. He's moving my car out of the no parking zone in front of the building."

"Your car? You drove here? From Saratoga?"

"I drove to Harrisburg, Pennsylvania, last night after I picked Candy and Mike up at the airport. Stayed at a Comfort Inn near there. Left at six this morning."

Candy and Mike's plane hadn't gotten into Albany until after seven. Mara counted the hours in her head. Four to Harrisburg. He must have gotten there about midnight. Another nine or so here. "Are you crazy?"

"Yes. About you." He grazed her cheek with his fingertips and slid his hand around to the tangle of curls at her neck.

She gripped his arm tighter to steady herself, and he crushed his lips to hers.

"Wow!" she said when he finished.

He took her hand and led her to the couch. "We have to talk."

Yeah. If she could get her lips or voice to work after that.

"I had a lot of time to think on the drive down."

Mara's senses began to return to normal. Candy! "Did Candy talk you into coming?" She didn't want him here because of anything Candy said or because he thought his family expected it of him.

"Candy didn't tell me anything I didn't already know. I had to see you. Tell you how much I love you. I realized I was being a jerk. Forget Saratoga. Forget my job. I need to be with you."

"You'd do that for me?" She didn't know her hands were shaking until he took them in his and stopped the trembling.

"No, for us."

Mara's insides melted into a pool of liquid warmth. Warmth she could have lost herself in if the slow, self-satisfied smile that followed his words hadn't set off an alarm in her head. After not calling her all week, he'd made a one-eighty turnaround. Before she could accept what he was saying, she had to be sure he meant it.

"Seriously, what about your law practice?"

"I'm sure T.J. and Jace will buy me out. And I have some leads on jobs from the conference last month."

The temperature dropped ten degrees. "Wait. You were looking at jobs here before Candy's wedding?"

"Yeah." Pink tinged his cheekbones. "Then I got scared. Okay?"

"You. Scared. Of what?"

"Of making another mistake. Leaving my comfort zone. Then my client mentioned the job at the Gideon. It seemed like—"

"The easy way out," she finished.

"Hey." He tapped her on the nose. "You know I wouldn't take that from anyone but you."

"I know." She cuddled up next to him. "It wasn't easy for me either to leave New York and everyone and move down here."

He twirled a lock of her hair around his finger interrupting her train of thought.

She shook her head free. "But that doesn't excuse the way you acted after the rehearsal dinner or on the way to the airport."

"What can I say? I'm a guy. Now can we kiss and make up?"

"No. One more question."

Concern flashed across his face. She shouldn't torture him like this, but it was so much fun.

"Alex Price, I love you. Will you marry me?"

"Yes," he answered in a low husky voice that sent a delicious shiver through her and set her heart to pounding so hard she thought she'd explode.

"On one condition."

Her chest tightened mid-heartbeat.

"I get to pick the honeymoon. I know a great cruise line."

She threw her arms around his neck and laughed. "Shut up and kiss me."